PETER SUTCLIFFE'S WAITING IN THE CORRIDOR

Tim Munro

Peter Sutcliffe's Waiting in the Corridor
Copyright © 2017 by Tim Munro. All Rights Reserved.

All rights reserved. No part of this book may be reproduced in any form or by any electronic or mechanical means including information storage and retrieval systems, without permission in writing from the author. The only exception is by a reviewer, who may quote short excerpts in a review.

Cover designed by Goya and Tim Munro

This book is a work of fiction. Names, characters, places, and incidents either are products of the author's imagination or are used fictitiously. Any resemblance to actual persons, living or dead, events, or locales is entirely coincidental.

Printed in the United States of America

First Printing: Aug 2017
Tim Munro

ISBN-9781698460628

PART ONE

THE CORRIDOR OF POWER

For Jack and Calum

Dave Hardman liked to arrive early for work. He enjoyed the quiet of the staff room before the ensuing onslaught of children arriving, and on this day especially, the first day back after half term. The fact that the words 'half term' were no longer applicable irritated him. There were now six terms not three, so half terms no longer existed, even though he'd just had a week off! That summed up the system, perfectly; changing labels didn't mean that anything was different at all. So, at six forty five, as he pulled off the main road and through the gates of Southgreen Academy, he was looking forward to Term Six, knowing that a summer of invigilating exams and watching cricket on the green lay ahead, with the school fair the anarchic climax, before the bliss of six weeks off.

He was humming as he switched off the CD player and Graham Nash's sweet voice stopped abruptly. He always played the Crosby, Stills, Nash and Young song about teaching children, as he drove to school. He'd seen them live at Wembley Stadium in 1974 and it reminded him of the idealism that had possessed him at that time. As a prologue to the day ahead, it tempered the cynicism that twenty five years of teaching had fostered.

"Hello, Mr Hardman," said Mr Doyle, as Dave got out of his Honda Accord. "Nearly beat me to it today. The ex-missus driving a hard bargain again, is she?"

Dave forced half a smile. He knew not to rise to the bait. The school caretaker was not one to rile. Mr Doyle knew only too well that the reason Dave was in school so early was to mark exam papers. The divorce had hit him hard and the extra money he made from the exam board, for moderating and marking, restored a measure of equilibrium. So he said nothing in reply and walked briskly to the staff room, where he made himself a coffee and settled down to work.

He concentrated resolutely. It wasn't just a money making exercise. Dave was truly committed and knew how important these exams were for the children. Their future was in his hands, so giving their work his full attention was paramount. He mumbled to himself as he marked, checking and double checking. He always loved it when he came across a paper of quality. "Clever lad," he whispered, as if the student was there listening, "don't befuddle your brain with too many drugs and who knows what you might achieve." He took a sip of coffee and picked up the next paper, as Brian Bull entered, clomping along in his Wellington boots.

"You're here early, aren't you, Mr Hardman?" Dave didn't respond. Like Mr Doyle, Mr Bull could be irritating.

"Please yourself." He meandered across to the notice board and gave it a cursory glance before heading for the photocopier.

Feeling slightly guilty, Dave said, "Sorry, Mr Bull, I didn't mean to –"

But Mr Bull chipped in with, "No, it's alright, I can see you're –"

"Marking. Yes. Exams"

"I can see. Only, Peter Sutcliffe's waiting in the corridor." The very mention of the name filled Dave with apprehension.

"This early?"

"Something about theatre tickets."

"Damn," said Dave, remembering his mistake.

"What?"

"I haven't sent for them."

"What?"

"The tickets. National Theatre. It's first come first served and Peter Sutcliffe always gets here early, so he's top of the list. He wants to see their production of ' 'Tis Pity She's a Whore.' "

"Well he would do wouldn't he? Right up his street," said Mr Bull, entering into the inevitable confusion surrounding the boy's name.

"There's a scheme you see, for young people but with all this I've ..."

"Balls'd it up?"

"Yes."

"I see."

"So could you?"

"Tell him to go away?"

Dave nodded.

"My pleasure," said Mr Bull, revelling in the impending task. He had no time for Peter Sutcliffe, no time at all, but then ... very few did.

Dave returned to his marking and, almost immediately, started to giggle but the giggling had turned to full blown laughter by the time Mr Bull returned.

"Here, listen to what this boy's written. 'I think Romeo fancies Juliet 'cos she's got nice tits. I agree with Romeo 'cos she did in the video. We rewound that bit but Miss took the remote away.'"

"I told him you weren't here but he said he'd seen your car."

"So?" said Dave.

"I told him not to be a cheeky little bleeder and next time he did Rural Science I'd dip his face in pig shit."

"Many thanks, Mr Bull but just 'cos you're the school farm manager and not a bog standard teacher like the rest of us, doesn't give you the authority to speak to students like that. What did he say?"

"That he was giving up Rural Science."

"What reason?"

"On principle."

"What principle?"

"He's become a vegetarian."

"Has he really? I'm impressed."

Mr Bull steamed on, "Gave me all this shite about animals having feelings and stuff like that."

"Don't they?" asked Dave.

"What?"

"Have feelings?"

"Don't you start," said Mr Bull, scornfully.

"The trouble with Peter Sutcliffe is, he's obsessive," said Dave.

"Of course he is," replied Mr Bull, compounding the confusion, "killing all those slappers!"

"And ... he's adolescent."

"Spotty even! And ginger!"

"That too," agreed Dave.

"Fancy being called that?"

"Sorry?"

"I mean, being called Sutcliffe and naming their son, Peter, after the Yorkshire Ripper, the biggest serial killer in this nation's history!"

Dave corrected him. "You're wrong there. It's lucky he wasn't called Shipman."

"But it was *Harold* Shipman not Peter," Mr Bull continued, "and anyway, he wasn't a celebrity murderer when our kid here was born. I'm talking about Peter Sutcliffe, the man who killed the tarts."

Dave bristled. "I think you'll find that they were women he killed. They certainly weren't all prostitutes. And prostitutes are human beings. Besides, perhaps Peter's granddad was called Peter."

Mr Bull was confused. "What?"

Dave was irritated now. "Is that all you ever say?"

"What?"

"There you go again."

"I don't –"

"Understand, I know! I mean Peter's dad. Maybe his dad was called Peter too. Perhaps he was a really good bloke and died or something and his son wanted to name the boy, Peter, in his memory. It's pretty common."

"What?"

"I don't believe this!"

"No, but what if they'd had a girl?" asked Mr Bull, swerving off at a tangent.

"What?" said Dave.

"You're saying it now!"

"What?"

"There, you've done it again!"

"What?" repeated Dave, aggressively.

Mr Bull looked triumphant. "That's three times now! Game, set and match! You gave me grief for saying 'what' and now you're saying it!"

"You're a prick!" said Dave.

"There's no need to be abusive."

"Oh yes, there is."

"I was only saying,"

"Yes, I know you were," and in his tone and the look that Brian Bull returned, they both agreed to back down. Mr Bull shuffled. He wanted to placate Dave so he came back with, "Look, want a turkey at Christmas for free?"

"No thanks," said Dave, curtly.

"I'll pluck it and everything."

"I prefer mine with feathers!"

"I've got loads of young'uns," added Mr Bull but Dave was having none of it.

"I think it's immoral!"

"What?"

"There you go again!"

"Sorry?"

"So am I," said Dave, before delivering the coup de grace. "I'm a vegan!"

Mr Bull was out of his depth. "Oh, shit, no, you mean ... you're a ..."

"Vegan, yes."

"And *you* think it's immoral?"

"Yes. All this Christmas turkey and fattening the calf in the name of education. Having a school farm and teaching children how to slaughter animals."

"But I love animals!" Mr Bull pleaded in mitigation.

"Oh, I wouldn't question that, Mr Bull."

But before he could go on, Dave started laughing loudly.

"What's so funny?" asked Mr Bull.

Dave could hardly get the words out, "I'm sorry it's just ... Mr *Bull ... Bull.*" But again the raucous laugh took over until he blurted out, "Did your dad know at your christening that you were going to be a cattle farmer, and that when the bottom fell out of the beef market, with all and sundry keeling over from mad cow disease, you'd become the local school farm manager?"

"I had to diversify."

"No question, but ... it's still funny!"

"I've heard them all before."

"What?"

"There, you said it again. The jokes about my name."

And now Dave couldn't resist pulling rank. "Well, perhaps you shouldn't make snide comments about other people's names."

"Whose?"

"Peter Sutcliffe's"

Contrite, Mr Bull replied, "I know. You're right. But would you credit it ...?"

"What?"

"There you go again. The Ripper; naming their son after the Yorkshire bloody Ripper. Any road, I've had enough dozy animals to deal with already this morning without having to listen to you."

"Sorry," said Dave.

"No you're not. And my father did know I'd be a cattle farmer. He was one too. So was his dad. I'm the last generation."

"I am sorry, really," said Dave trying to smooth things over but immediately his tongue got the better of him, "I know you do a good job, it's just ... I don't like *what* you do. I expect there were many Germans who said the same about the SS!"

"Now that's –"

"Flippant hyperbole but it's a point worth making ... what?"

Mr Bull didn't understand but looked shocked anyway. He'd had enough, "I'm off!"

"Okay."

"You're too quick for me."

Trying to be helpful, Dave reminded him, "Your photocopying?"

But Brian Bull didn't care. "It'll wait," he said and left.

Dave settled down again to mark, chuckling to himself, thinking, "Vegetarian indeed, that's a turn up for the books. Peter and me batting for the same side, eh?" But as he picked up another exam paper to mark, Julia Lyons came bounding in, wearing a bright yellow track suit and taking herself and Dave by surprise.

"Oh, hello, I didn't expect to see anyone here so early"

"No. I'm marking exam papers. The first batch from this year's GCSEs. A few extra quid. Kids. Alimony. Two mortgages. Child support. You know how it is."

"No," replied Julia.

"Didn't think you would. You'll find out," said Dave cynically. "Anyway, I thought your student placement finished at half term?"

"We don't say half term now. It's banned."

"I stand corrected."

"But I did leave. It's just –" she faltered.

"Yes?"

"I left some kit here."

"With Andy? It doesn't surprise me."

"Sorry?"

"Andy. Head of PE."

Julia was embarrassed and tongue tied, "No, it's just …"

"It's alright, I *know*," said Dave, pointedly.

"Know what?" said Julia, feigning innocence.

"About Andy."

"And?"

"Everything," said Dave, knowingly.

"Do you?"

"Yes."

"How?"

"No matter," said Dave, not giving anything away. I think you'd better wait for him, er…"

"Elsewhere?"

"If you don't mind," said Dave, "then, perhaps, I can get some of this bloody marking done."

"Of course. Sorry."

"No matter. Mum's the word."

Julia hurried out. Dave looked at the clock. It was 07.35 and he'd only marked two papers. So much for his early start. As he gulped the last dregs of cold coffee, he muttered to himself, "Randy Andy, up to his old tricks again."

◆ ◆ ◆

As Julia hurried along the corridor towards Andy's office she had no idea that his nickname was used by many members of staff. She was under the impression that the rather unoriginal, Randy Andy was her own personal name for him and, in the preceding two terms of her teaching practice, she hadn't missed any opportunity to get him to live up to his title. They had even played a sex game where Andy pretended to be the current Duke of York (who'd had to bear the same burden for years) and they would joyfully sing the children's nursery rhyme as they marched around Andy's personal shower room. It gave new meaning to the lines, "When they were up they were up and when they were down they were down." Sometimes Andy would sing this as he removed Julia's knickers and she would reciprocate pulling down his boxer shorts before they would burst into laughter with, "And when they were only halfway up, they were neither up nor down."

They often had sex early in the morning, before the children arrived but, if the truth be known, they weren't restricted by any notion of time. As Head of PE Andy had his own office, which led, through a door, to a tiled changing area with a bench, a few lockers and an opaque glass, shower cubicle. Andy guarded the key to his office with his life and only grudgingly lent it to his deputy, Dick Fenwick, when his number two needed to shower which was, thankfully for Andy, only on rare occasions, since personal hygiene wasn't one of Dick's strong points.

But, on this first day of the new term, Andy wasn't expecting Julia. She was back at college, or so he thought. They hadn't seen each other in the week off, as Julia had been playing in a tennis competition in Eastbourne and Andy had been away with some ex-school friends, for most of the week, at a secret stag party in Amsterdam, that became extended after the prospective groom was found stark naked, chained to a lamppost, outside a brothel in the red light district. This was run of the mill stuff for the famously tolerant Dutch police, who were used to the ever errant British. They rescued the nude groom (now having doubts about his choice of Andy as best man) and looked after him as if he were a stolen exhibit from the Rijksmuseum, but the paperwork meant that the stags missed their flight home.

So when there was a knock at Andy's office door he responded with, "Won't be a sec, Dick," before he heard the loud whisper from Julia saying, "It's not Dick, it's me!"

Andy opened the door immediately and, as he pulled Julia towards him, they kissed with a passion that only a week apart could arouse.

"How was Eastbourne?" asked Andy.

"I missed you," said Julia.

"Did you?" asked Andy.

"Yes!"

They kissed again.

"How was the stag do?"

"Quite subdued really. Exeter's a quiet place." (Andy never liked Julia knowing his exact whereabouts.) "We tried to get the groom to shag a sheep but he was too pissed on cider to manage it. But everyone got completely rat arsed."

Julia presented her rear to Andy and started gyrating her hips, saying, "Talking of which."

Andy needed no encouragement, pressing his crotch against her bum and fondling her breasts, as she said, "Did you really miss me?"

"Of course."

But she wanted firmer confirmation, "Did you?"

"I said."

"I know," replied Julia and they kissed again. They started to undress and Andy reached across, turning on the power shower. Julia started to sing 'The Grand Old Duke of York' but Andy stopped her with a kiss, saying, "No time for that, babe." Both naked now, he pulled her into the hot, steaming shower, as Julia said,

"I've wanted you so much!"

"Don't talk," said Andy.

"We must," said Julia.

"About?"

"The future."

"Don't," said Andy.

"Our future."

"Not now, babe. It's 7.45. All the staff and kids will be arriving presently. This is definitely not the time."

"Now I'm back at college, I just wanted to know –"

"Well you know the old saying?" said Andy.

"No," said Julia, "what?"

They kissed with renewed passion as the water and steam engulfed their bodies and Andy pushed down on Julia's shoulders, so she was kneeling before him as he said,

"The proof of the pudding …"

As the steaming water and heat intensified, Julia giggled, understanding his meaning absolutely and said, "Oh, Andy. You do say the nicest things!" Then she could do nothing other than comply with his oh, so, very early, morning request.

♦ ♦ ♦

Sebastian Swinton had a new title. Under the recently appointed Principal, he was now known as the Vice Principal, though for years he'd been known as the Deputy Head. His job description however hadn't changed one iota. As Dave would have it, this came under the 'half term' category of nonsense.

Sebastian's nickname was Basil, as he had the distinct, woebegone air of the infamous patron of Fawlty Towers, though few would call him this to his face. Everybody knew that if Basil wasn't there, the almighty edifice of Southgreen would crumble within days but, thankfully, Basil was always there, as he prided himself on never having had a day off through sickness in over twenty five years.

The summer was a particularly challenging time for him, as it was always a nightmare compiling the timetable for the next academic year, especially when he could never be sure who would be teaching what, to whom, where. Other than that, he was always having to cope with excluding badly behaved pupils, not to mention disciplining badly behaved staff and generally trying, and usually failing, to make everything run smoothly.

There was also the new technology. Computers were a constant source of irritation to him. It might be halfway through the first decade of the twenty first century but he wished he was back in the 1960s where there wasn't a CD ROM in sight. The school systems were constantly crashing and the IT consultant, knocked off at midday. The newly installed computerised, interactive whiteboards were a waste of time and money, in his opinion, and why teachers couldn't just stick to chalk and blackboards was a mystery to him. For him the ordinary plastic, classroom whiteboards and whiteboard marker pens were already one innovation too far. The pens were messy and, even worse, sometimes indelible and you couldn't throw them at students like you could with a good, old fashioned piece of chalk.

You'd be hard pushed to find any member of staff who really liked Sebastian, as he just wasn't really the likeable type. Dave tolerated him, reluctantly, as he knew that the school couldn't function without him. Constantly harassed, he was prone to fits of temper. But he had one characteristic that endeared him to most people. He had to curb the habit now, with the new Principal in place but, other than that, he didn't care who heard. Sebastian couldn't stop swearing.

"Fucking Linda's off again" he said, disturbing Dave's marking, as he entered the staff room carrying some papers.

"PMT?" enquired Dave, as this was Linda's usual excuse.

"She's supposed to be a member of the SMT!"

Always one to defend a colleague Dave said, "Granted she's one of the Senior Management Team but perhaps her PMT is preventing her from carrying out her SMT responsibilities."

"It's not fucking PMT," said Sebastian.

"What is it, then?" asked Dave.

"She's totally fucking depressed!"

Dave couldn't resist it. "Well, you would be too if you had her job: Head of Maths in a rural comprehensive where counting is measured in sheep."

"And Peter fucking Sutcliffe's waiting in the corridor. Something about theatre tickets. That's your department as Head of English and the fucking Performing Arts."

Dave got out of his chair. He strode over to the filing cabinet and pulled out a wad of forms, tearing one off and handing it to Sebastian.

"So, a referral form. What's this supposed to mean? If you've got a fucking axe to grind about detention duty you can fuck off!"

"Seven," said Dave.

"Sorry?"

"That's seven 'fucks' in the last thirty seconds."

"So, you a fucking prude?" said Sebastian, thinking Dave should have grown used to his mode of speech by now.

"No," said Dave, "but these forms for student detentions have boxes we have to tick and one of them says, 'obscene and offensive language.'"

"So fucking what?"

"Irony, Seb?"

"Fuck irony. There's a time and a place for swearing and it's not in the fucking classroom!"

"But the staff room's fine?"

"Fucking fine by me."

"But you're the Deputy Head!"

"Vice Principal now, please, and I've got the fucking scars to prove it. Anyway that fucking Linda woman's doing my head in. I've booked a supply teacher who only has maths, grade 'C' GCSE and his speciality is fucking Drama!"

"He'll do."

"Yes, but can he fucking count?"

And with that Sebastian headed for the Principal's office, becoming suddenly absorbed in the papers he was holding. He was good at multi-tasking. He stopped at the door and turned back to Dave.

"Is the boss in yet?"

"No. Here, you don't want to be swearing in front of her," said Dave, showing a degree of concern.

"I don't," said Seb, reassuringly. "Oh, the odd 'bugger' or 'bloody' slips out but I've managed to control it."

"So, why can't you control it with the rest of us?"

"Habit. Anyway, everybody's used to it. Just one of those things."

"Strange."

"Yes ... fucking strange. Is Helga in yet?"

"No. She's working to rule."

"What?" said Seb, worried.

"Hates the boss. Never gets in a moment before she has to now. She was always half an hour early with old Foulkes."

"You mean Helga's rebelling?"

"Aren't we all, Seb," now adding to the Vice Principal's worries.

"Seriously, Dave, don't say that. This is supposed to be a new start. As one of the first schools with Academy status we need to be setting an example." And with that Sebastian turned about face and headed out of the staff room.

Dave sat down again, thinking that Sebastian had a funny way of showing exemplary behaviour, since every sentence he uttered was littered with expletives. He started to pack the exam papers into his briefcase, when Helga appeared and crossed to the Principal's Office, surveying the sign on the door, in passing.

"Morning Dave."

"Morning, Helga."

"She's not going to like that," said Helga, laughing.

"What?" asked Dave.

"Ms Sedgeford asked Mr Doyle to change the sign from 'Head Teacher' to 'Principal's Office' when she arrived eight weeks ago."

"I could have sworn I saw him doing that over half term, when I came in to pick up my marking."

"Oh, he did it alright," said Helga. "Just a pity you didn't take it upon yourself to supervise him, Dave, being Head of English."

"Sorry?"

"Well, come and have a look."

Dave joined Helga by the door and there, in beautifully gold painted signwriting, on a jet black background, were the words: 'Principles Office.'

Helga and Dave laughed together. They both knew that Mr Doyle was, as they say, 'academically challenged.'

"He's spelt it wrong," confirmed Helga.

"And, even then he's left an apostrophe out," said Dave. "He's going to take some stick for this. I can't wait! Careful though, Helga; the boss is going to be in a foul mood when she sees it."

"No change there, then."

"It's that bad is it?" asked Dave, returning to his chair.

"Worse," said Helga as she entered the office and closed the door. She hung her jacket on the hook and picked up some correspondence from her desk. Then she crossed to the adjoining door that led to the Principal's part of the office and opened it, checking that the new Principal hadn't already arrived and entered through the other door that linked her room direct to the corridor. The coast was clear. She switched the kettle on. She had her own kitchen area so that she didn't have to compete with the chaos of the staff room, especially at busy times. She turned on the radio. The Boomtown Rats' song about not liking Mondays, boomed out. Even though it was Tuesday and she agreed totally with the sentiment, she switched it off, as she knew that Ms Sedgeford couldn't abide Radio 1 and had already asked her not to tune into that particular station. She didn't like modern music. She preferred Classic FM or if she was trying to impress a visitor, BBC Radio 3. Helga knew it was all for show. Ever since she had taken over the job at Easter, she'd rubbed everybody up the wrong way. Helga knew that change was needed to chivvy up a staff who had become set in their ways, but the kind of change that Bethany Sedgeford was bringing in was change just for the sake of it, in Helga's opinion.

Helga put a spoonful of coffee into her cup, and was just filling it with boiling water, when the door opened and in walked Ms Sedgeford. She was a dark haired, imposing looking woman, in her late forties. If someone had described her as a Thatcherite clone morphed into New Labour, they wouldn't have been far off the mark. She oozed self-confidence, but concealed beneath the surface lay a definite vulnerability.

"Tea break first thing on a Monday, Helga?"

"It does feel like a Monday, I'll grant you but it's actually Tuesday."

"So it is. These bank holidays kick everything out of kilter."

"Anyway, it's coffee and I think you'll find I'm early."

"I know you do a marvellous job, Helga," said Bethany in her usual patronising tone, "but are those coffee granules politically correct? Probably grown by some poor peasant who is trying to support his wife and twelve kids, while he's being ripped off by the coffee house culture in London and poor, unsuspecting people like yourself."

"I only have Gold Blend," said Helga.

"Yes and Gold Blend standards need to be maintained. We all have to strive to achieve them if we are to shine as one of the new academies. That's why I was appointed as Principal."

"Yes, Mrs Sedgeford."

"Ms, Helga; I keep on telling you, Ms"

"I know, *Ms* Sedgeford."

"When Tony and I get married I'll tell you. You'll get a piece of wedding cake like everyone else."

"Would you like a herbal before the briefing?"

"I think there's just about time," said Bethany, adding, "you're so thoughtful, Helga."

"I try to be. Camomile or Elderflower?"

"Elderflower, please. I wouldn't want you to think that your efforts aren't appreciated but, Helga, we must move with the times."

"Of course, Ms Sedgeford."

"You're learning, Helga, and that's what this establishment is all about."

"Yes, Ms Sedgeford."

"I have been here nearly two months now, Helga. I've told you before, it's quite alright for you to call me Bethany when we're on our own."

Outside the door, Sebastian could hardly believe his eyes, seeing the result of Mr Doyle's brilliant craftsmanship but useless spelling. He knocked anyway.

"Come in," said Bethany.

Sebastian put his head round the door. "Sorry to bother you boss but Peter Sutcliffe's waiting in the corridor."

"Yes?" replied Bethany, with a look of concern. She might only have been the incumbent for a few weeks but that had been long enough for Peter Sutcliffe to inhabit her dreams with his constant pestering.

"Something about being School Council rep and being a vegetarian. He's trying to make a moral point about the school farm, I think. I told him to bugger off - I mean go away - but he insists on seeing you."

"Tell him to go away again would you please, Sebastian. It's not the time or the place, either for your bad language or Peter Sutcliffe's constant, unnecessary enquiries. He knows very well that the School Council meets every six weeks and there's not another forum until the thirtieth."

"Okay. You doing the briefing? First day back after half term and all that."

"Of course I am, Sebastian. And how many times do I have to tell you, half terms don't exist anymore!"

"No, I know they don't. Slip of the -"

"It's the start of term six. We had a week off at the end of term five and an extra day for the bank holiday, which I trust you enjoyed Sebastian?"

"Oh, yes, boss, it was absolute fu-" but Sebastian stopped himself just in time and started coughing in a most exaggerated way. "Sorry boss, frog in the throat. I was going to say it was total and absolute *fun*, sitting in my study, on a boiling hot, summer's day, getting my head round the timetable for next year. But then that's normal for me at Whitsun."

"Alright, Sebastian you don't have to play the martyr on my behalf. I know how hard you work."

"I take it you've seen the new sign, boss?"

"What sign, Sebastian?"

"The sign on your door that you've been badgering Mr Doyle about since you arrived."

"No, I hadn't noticed," said Bethany, smiling. You mean he's finally got round to doing it? Splendid!"

"I don't think you'll be saying that when you see it, boss."

"Why?" asked Bethany, as Sebastian pushed the door open revealing Mr Doyle's pristine handiwork.

"I don't believe it," said Bethany, expressing both shock and rage. "The imbecile! Helga, get on the phone to Mr Doyle and say if he's not at the briefing in two minutes I won't be held responsible for my actions. I've got vital meetings with primary heads this morning!" And with that, Bethany Sedgeford retreated into the safety of her office, slamming the door behind her. Sebastian looked at Helga, raising an eyebrow. She smiled and giggled. He hit his forehead.

♦ ♦ ♦

The support staff were always the first to arrive at the morning briefing. These were the classroom assistants who did a fantastic job. Everyone knew that without them the children really would be left high and dry. They had a closer relationship with the pupils than the teachers did, partly because some of them were assigned to work with individual students with learning or, more often, behavioural difficulties. But the children also actually enjoyed feelings of empathy with them. It was as if they were cut from the same cloth. Some of them had probably had similar battles with under achievement, which is why they were now classroom assistants, and this earned them a measure of respect. The children's behaviour however could be extremely challenging and they bore the brunt of it. Despite this, they were totally undervalued for all their hard work, even though Senior Management conspired to pretend that they weren't. They were grossly underpaid and by now had become so harassed, downtrodden and disillusioned that they had almost given in. They would sit in the same chairs at the briefing every morning and not say a word, except on the rare occasions when their spokesperson, a timid, blonde woman by the name of Susan Shepherd, would mention something on their behalf. Her voice however, was so quiet and shrill and her delivery so unsure and nervous that, frankly, she'd have been better advised never to have uttered a syllable, as no one could hear or understand a word she ever said. Consequently, the conditions of work of the support staff never changed and none of the few suggestions they made were ever acted upon, except perhaps when they begrudgingly volunteered (because none of the teachers would) for stints, with wrists locked, in the stocks at the Summer Fair, when soaking sponges, along with all manner of other, unmentionable objects were hurled at them. So, as they gathered at the briefing at the start of the new term, in the orderly rows of chairs where they sat, a visitor might easily have mistaken them for dummies, like mannequins they'd find in the window of any department store in the country, or wax works at Madame Tussauds.

They were in good company however but could never really compete with a member of staff who, unlike them, was at the very top of the pecking order. Mr Hill was the Head of Science and, rather like his parliamentary equivalent, was known as the Father of the School, for he was the oldest and longest serving member of staff. He could have retired years ago and, if the truth be told, the old Head Teacher, Mr Foulkes, had offered him extra incentives to do so, but this only served to stiffen Mr Hill's resolve to remain in situ. And remain in situ he did. Until, that is, the arrival of the new Principal, when Mr Hill decided that his time was up and the staff were informed of his imminent retirement, at the end of the summer term.

At almost any time (for he did little teaching these days) he could be found fast asleep in his personal, reclining chair, in a quiet corner of the staff room. For Mr Hill suffered from the unfortunate and debilitating condition of narcolepsy, which meant that he could fall asleep quite suddenly and not be woken by any external stimulation or encouragement. He could snap out of it, equally as quickly apparently, though no one could ever recall actually witnessing this. Added to this chronic disability, he also suffered from the added complication of cataplexy, which caused his muscles to lose all strength and resulted in a temporary total inability to move. This could be quite frightening if a stranger, who wasn't used to Mr Hill and his drowsy ways, encountered him in his chair, for he or she might readily assume that Mr Hill was dead!

So, as Bethany Sedgeford stood up to start the briefing, the last couple of teachers arrived, muttering apologies and the support staff sat like dummies, in their neat, orderly rows, while Mr Hill lay motionless in his chair.

"Firstly, I hope you all had a good break," said Bethany, but before she could continue she was halted by Dave, interrupting. Dave hated the briefings which were, in his opinion, a total waste of time. It was his personal crusade to use any excuse to disrupt them and the first word that Bethany had spoken had given him just the opportunity.

"You can't have 'firstly,' it's bad grammar."

"Sorry, Mr Hardman?" said Bethany, taken aback.

"It should be *first*, secondly, thirdly and so on," continued Dave. "A minor point but since my department are getting endless directives about teaching good grammar and doing away with the liberal ideas of the 1960s, I thought it my duty to point it out. Start at the top so to speak."

Bethany could scarcely hide her irritation but responded by saying, "Thank you, Dave for pointing it out," the use of his first name being a signal to the staff that they were really good mates, when they demonstrably weren't.

"As I was saying, I hope you've all come back refreshed and raring to go. The most important item relates to Tesco coupons that we have been saving for special resources for the science department. Mr Hill will fill you in on this. Mr Hill?"

And, quick as a flash, just as was usual, Mr Hill was saved embarrassment by his deputy; a toadying, rather boring but well-meaning Welshman, by the name of Mr Dylan, who always spoke up on his behalf. Indeed, in reality, it was Mr Dylan who ran the science department and wanted the job officially.

"Mr Hill has flagged this my way. I'd just ask group tutors –"

"Mr Dylan, you're living in the past," said Bethany, correcting him. "It's mentors now and has been since we became a new academy at Easter."

"Sorry, Ms Sedgeford," replied Mr Dylan. "Well if mentors could send students in their tutor, sorry, mentor group who have collected coupons, to the science lab at one o'clock today. This is the last chance saloon."

Bethany went on, stressing the first word, "*Secondly*, may I remind you, I will be meeting primary school heads this morning and that any queries should go to Helga in the office. *Thirdly*, there's a special, full staff meeting at 3.45 today to discuss the possible forthcoming inspection. I expect all staff to attend this very important brainstorming session. Has anyone got anything to say?"

Dave had. He couldn't resist it. "Yes, Ms Sedgeford, I think brainstorming sounds a potentially hazardous and dangerous exercise and I'll be asking my union rep to look into the health and safety aspects. Could you explain exactly what this brainstorming session will entail?"

Confident in herself, Bethany replied, "Well, *first*, as you well know, Dave, it's a word that's commonly used in all areas of the educational community and, *secondly*, as Head of English I think you're being rather naughty here, as it's plain to everyone what I mean, isn't it? Don't you agree?" There were murmurs of agreement from other teachers but Bethany looked for more vocal support. "Mr Hill, as Father of the School, you know what brainstorming means don't you?" But she was barking up the wrong tree and Mr Dylan, once more, came to Mr Hill's aid.

"We use it all the time in science and recognise its definite educational merits, vis-a-vis methods of experimentation."

"Thank you, Mr Dylan," replied Bethany, "but I'm sure Mr Hill can speak for himself, he's been brainstorming for years, haven't you, Mr Hill?"

"Brain dead more like," said Dave, audibly under his breath.

"Sorry, Mr Hardman?" said Bethany, darting Dave a daggers' look, but he was saved by the bell for what was now called, 'Mentoring Registration.' "Thank you Mr Hill. Any questions from the support staff? Susan?" Susan blushed. "No, as usual. Have a day of invigorating learning everyone and I'll see you all at 3.45."

As the staff were dispersing however, Mr Doyle appeared in the doorway. Bethany Sedgeford pounced like a lioness and her eyes gleamed with the prospect of playing with and clawing at her prey. "Mr Doyle, so good of you to have graced us with your presence, albeit so late in the proceedings. Eight weeks ago I asked you to change the sign on my office door and -"

"You'll be pleased to hear I've done it Ms Sedgeford," interrupted Mr Doyle, proudly. He still had no idea of what he'd done wrong, Helga having failed to inform him of the exact nature of his summons.

"Done it? Oh, yes, you've been and gone and done it alright! But what about the spelling, eh, Mr Doyle? You couldn't get into the lowest set in Year 7 with spelling as bad as that, you cretin! Didn't you think of checking it first, you total imbecile? Now get in my office right now!" And with that, Bethany stormed out, fuming, into her office and Mr Doyle followed, shuffling past Dave, who muttered, "It's the principle of the thing, I think you'll find's the problem." But Mr Doyle was still none the wiser and, as he entered the Principal's office, giving his handiwork a quizzical look and closing the door behind him, the rest of the staff heard every word of the terrible abuse that the poor caretaker had to suffer, caught in the unretracted claws of the furious feline.

◆ ◆ ◆

The staff room was suddenly empty. That is, until a young man entered looking lost, flustered and somewhat out of breath. He was holding an identity badge, which he'd not yet hung round his neck, saying, 'Visitor.' He looked about eighteen but was actually twenty four and was called Tom Carter. He stood holding a tatty briefcase and looked lost. He crossed to a table and picked up a copy of the Times Educational Supplement. He stared at it but replaced it immediately. Helga entered the staff room from her office and put a document into the photocopier.

"Hello," she said.

"Hello," said Tom.

"Are you the supply?"

"Yes."

"For Miss Baker?"

"Head of Maths?"

"That's right."

"It's a Mr Swinton I have to see."

"He'll be along in a minute," replied Helga, reassuringly. She picked up her photocopying.

"It's just I got lost on the A two five –"

"Don't worry."

"I'm late."

"No matter, there's some time before the first lesson. Miss Baker doesn't have a mentor group so you don't have to register students. Sebastian will be here presently."

"Sebastian?"

"Mr Swinton," explained Helga, adding, "Would you like a cup of tea?"

"Would coffee be possible?" ventured Tom.

"Not a problem."

"Thanks so much."

"Not at all," said Helga as she went back into the office and started to make the coffee."

Bethany's door opened. "Another cup of coffee, Helga?"

"It's for the supply."

"Who's sick today?"

"Linda."

"Again?

"Depression apparently."

"Far be it from me to gossip, Helga," (though it was obvious that she revelled in it) "but the word is, it's all because Andy in PE dumped her a few weeks ago."

"She wouldn't be the first," said Helga, who, although the wrong side of forty and more than ten years older than Andy, had herself rebuffed his unwelcome advances on more than one occasion.

"She's trying it on, Helga," said Bethany. "First it was PMT and period pain and when the doctor realised she was having the longest periods in the history of female suffering it became plain depression."

"The supply's nervous," said Helga.

"They generally are," replied Bethany. "When's my first primary head expected?"

"Mr Sanders from Brooksham at 9.30. Then you've got Mr Hartley from Broad Oak and Mrs. McAuliffe from Clayhurst. Then it's Mr Amyes from -"

"Stop, or you'll confuse me," said Bethany. "Right, I better get prepared." And with that Bethany looked in the mirror and started preening herself.

"The more students we can get into the first year, the more money we'll have. It's absolutely essential that we can get the local primary heads to see the potential of sending their students here. Our intake is critical. It's a numbers game, Helga and our numbers are down. Show the first one in when he arrives."

"Yes, Ms Sedgeford," replied Helga as she finished making the supply teacher's coffee.

♦ ♦ ♦

Down in the depths of the PE department Andy Bailey stood before a group of Year 10 boys that included Peter Sutcliffe. "Valuables. Valuables in the box," he said, shaking it. "Mr Fenwick's on his way out there so I want you all on the upper field at the speed of light and before you say anything, Sutcliffe, I know it's 186,000 miles per second. Wayne, Miriam, Maxine and John, thank you; you take the bibs and the cones. Usual routine; run twice round the field when you get there." With this the children moved off and Andy shouted after them, "And if I see anyone chucking grass clippings it's a straight one hour after school!"

He returned to his office and made certain to close the door behind him, as he'd already let Françoise Poitin in, and the French teacher, who'd recently arrived at Southgreen on placement, was waiting for him, naked in the shower. Neither, Julia nor the depressed head of maths, Linda, knew that Andy had been two timing them both for weeks and Françoise was none the wiser either, because Andy had told her that both Linda and Julia were flings that meant nothing and were over. Andy was a past master at deception. He had no scruples.

"Bonjour, mon amour," said Francoise. "It's been too long."

"Don't talk," said Andy, "I haven't got long."

"That's a pity," she replied, "because I'm free period one." She emerged dripping wet from the shower and kissed him. She slid down his body, quickly pulling down his shorts and began giving him oral sex.

"Oh, yes! Très bien. Très bien," he said but was startled by a knock on the office door.

"You in there, Andy? It's only me." Relieved to hear a male voice, rather than the possibility of it being Julia returning, Andy replied, "Coming, Dick."

"You'd better be quick."

"Oh, I will be don't worry," said Andy, enjoying the subterfuge nearly as much as Françoise was relishing the task in hand.

"Thing is," shouted Dick, "Wayne Clark's just stuck an orange traffic cone on Peter Sutcliffe's head. It's wedged completely tight and he's screaming."

"Send him to Basil, he'll sort it out. I'm coming," replied Andy who got carried away and exclaimed, "très bien!"

"You alright in there?"

"Oh, yes. Yes! I'm covering French after break. Just practising my vocab," said Andy, smiling down at Françoise and finishing off with, "Très bien! Très bien, Mademoiselle!"

◆ ◆ ◆

As the Vice Principal entered the staff room, Tom Carter said, "I'm waiting for -" but couldn't get to the end of the sentence as Sebastian, looking angry, cut him off with, "Well, wait in the corridor will you! How many times do I have to tell you sixth formers that you are not allowed in the staff room on any account. Just because you get the privilege of mooching around in mufti all day -"

"But -"

"Don't you 'but' me or you'll find yourself doing a two hour after school detention!"

"I'm the supply teacher," said Tom. "Maths. Mr Carter."

"You mean?"

"Yes," confirmed Tom.

"I'm most terribly sorry, Mr Carter, you don't look old enough; do forgive me," said Sebastian.

"That's quite alright," replied Tom, though it wasn't. At college, Tom had been worried about his youthful looks and whether he'd ever have any authority over teenagers.

Sebastian tried to make light of it, but his analogy was in questionable taste. "Don't worry, after a few days at Southgreen you'll be sprouting grey hairs and your face will look as lined as W.H.Auden's."

"It's that bad, is it?"

"Worse. After a few weeks it'll look like W.H.Auden's bollocks!"

Tom, who loved Auden's poetry, was visibly shocked but Sebastian eased his fears to a degree, saying, "Only joking. Now, maths ... as a graduate of drama you'll be able to cope. You got grade 'C' at GCSE I see."

"Yes."

"Yes, well, if the little buggers can emulate you, we'll be doing alright in the league tables, eh? If they get bored you can do a bit of drama with them. Make a human calculator or something. Where have you taught before?"

"Nowhere."

"Sorry?" said a puzzled Sebastian.

Tom explained, "That is, nowhere full time. I just do supply. Actually, this is my very first day. You see, I'm an actor really."

"Oh, you're an actor really," said Sebastian, intrigued. "What sort of acting's that then? Walk on stuff? Extra work?"

"No, I've done some quite good things."

"Like what?"

"Theatre, radio, TV."

Sebastian wanted to know more. "TV, fascinating. What exactly?"

"Well I did an episode of 'The Bill.' "

Excited now, Sebastian said, " 'The Bill,' I never miss it. What did you play?"

Tom didn't want to go further but did, replying, "Well, nothing really. I mean it was a good part but I'd rather not say."

But Sebastian was having none of it. "Policeman or villain?"

"Villain."

"I thought so, you've got a shifty look about you. Murderer, thief, bank robber, what?"

"Well actually, I was, erm –" stuttered Tom.

"Don't be shy now, I won't tell anyone, I promise," said Sebastian.

"I was a paedophile."

With a look of total delight, Sebastian said, "A paedophile. A fucking child molester! Just the ticket. You'll get on swimmingly in this neck of the woods!"

Helga came in to do some photocopying, disturbing their conversation but Sebastian wanted to be first to tell her the news.

"Helga, you'll never believe it. We have a celebrity in our midst. Mr Carter here's an actor and he was in 'The Bill,' playing the part of a paedophile."

"Oh, how interesting," said Helga, though she wasn't entirely sure that was the right thing to say. Tom on the other hand, made a mental note never to trust Sebastian again, as he'd broken his promise within seconds of making it. But the undependable Basil wanted more information.

"How long ago was this then, Mr Carter?"

"About six months ago," said Tom.

"I do remember an excellent episode where the main CID man, you know the one, hard as nails, broke down and wept because he'd seen this poor girl in the most parlous state. It wasn't that one was it?"

"Yes, that was it."

"You mean you were the –?"

"Yes."

"You were the bastard who –"

"Mr Swinton!" Helga interrupted, feeling that Sebastian had gone too far.

"Yes," said Tom, reaffirming his role in the sordid affair.

"Well you deserved all you got. I'd lock them all up and throw away the fucking keys!"

"Mr Swinton, really!" said Helga, disapprovingly.

Tom now felt he had to not only defend himself but the character that he had played too, which wasn't very wise. "If you remember," he said, "he'd been badly abused himself as a child."

"That's what they all say. I don't care. He had no right. That poor, young, slip of a girl. Pretty, innocent young thing. Castration's too good for people like that. You're lucky to survive with your wedding tackle."

"Yes, he was," said Tom, trying to draw a distinct line between himself and the sexual deviant he had played.

"I wouldn't have recognised you. Couldn't have picked you out from an identity parade."

"No," said Tom, "my hair was different."

"Gave you the old paedo cut, I shouldn't wonder," said Sebastian. "Still it was a fucking good episode, so I suppose you should be proud. Wouldn't let the little buggers in 9CW find out though. They're merciless."

"My first class?" asked Tom, nervously.

"Yes," said Sebastian, adding, "well can't stand here chatting all day, the bell went ages ago. Here's a map of how to get to room 42. It's the other side of the school, so you'd better hurry. If you need any help ask the head of department or someone else down there in Maths."

Slightly confused, Tom said, "Right, but I thought ..." but was stopped by Sebastian saying, "Chop, chop, they'll be halfway up the wall by now" and ushering him out of the door.

Helga thought the foul mouthed Vice Principal needed reminding and said, "It's the Head of Maths, Miss Baker, who's away!"

"Don't talk to me about that skiver, Helga. She's had more sick notes than Stephen fucking Hawking!"

"Mr Swinton, that really is uncalled for. Mr Hawking's the most brilliant scientist and campaigner and that's no way to talk about a disabled genius. Anyway Miss Baker's depressed."

"I should cocoa"

"And she's *not here today*," repeated Helga.

"Do I look as if I need reminding?"

"But you told Mr Carter to see the Head of Department!"

"If he can find her, Helga. If he can find her."

He turned to leave the staff room but suddenly both he and Helga heard what can only be described as an animalistic howling coming from the corridor. He poked his head round the door only to be encountered by the last thing he wanted to see on this already, troublesome morning.

"Sutcliffe!" he bellowed. "What the hell are you doing with an orange traffic cone stuck to your matching, ginger head?" But Peter couldn't answer because he was in pain and simply continued howling. Sebastian, the epitome of sympathetic understanding, then warned him, shouting, "And don't you give me any lip. If you're not out of my sight and in the medical room before I can say 'lubrication' you'll be staying in for an hour after school! Lub-ri-ca!" but before he could get to the end of the word Peter Sutcliffe had gone.

Sebastian turned back into the staff room to Helga and said, "That'll teach him to murder prostitutes."

He was just about to leave to check that Peter Sutcliffe had indeed made his way to the medical room when he encountered a tall man entering the staff room. Acidly, he asked, "Can I help? Have you been to reception?"

"There was no one there," replied the tall man.

"Mr Swinton" said Helga, "I think – "

"Not now, Helga," said Sebastian, who was rather put off by the man towering over him and so admonished him with, "You should have a visitor's badge on."

"I'm sorry, I – "

But Sebastian cut in, saying, "You can't be too careful nowadays; gunmen, paedophiles, suicide bombers – "

"Yes, I know," said the visitor.

"Bloody maniacs all over the place," continued Sebastian. "I blame it on the parents. I'm sorry, who did you say you were?"

"I didn't. Mr Sanders, Head of Brooksham Primary, here to see Ms Sedgeford."

Sebastian changed immediately into his, Basil like, totally ingratiating self, feigning confusion by saying, "Oh, Mr *Sanders*. Of course, how silly of me. You should have said and then we could have dispensed with the niceties. Do forgive me. Ms Sedgeford is expecting you, do come through. I'll be off now if that's alright. Helga will look after you." And indeed, Helga did, while Sebastian made a hasty retreat and vanished.

Mr Sanders was visibly relieved.

"You'll have to forgive Mr Swinton," said Helga, "he's under a lot of pressure at the moment."

"I can see."

"Would you like a cup of tea or coffee, Mr Sanders?"

"Coffee, no sugar, please."

"Certainly. I'll percolate it," said Helga. Not just Gold Blend for this important visitor. "Do come through."

Helga led Mr Sanders through the door to the office, trying to distract him from the mess that had been made by Mr Doyle, prizing off the offending sign, immediately after his dressing down. She ushered him across to the adjoining door to Bethany's office and knocked.

"Come in," said Bethany and Mr Sanders did so. "How good of you to come. Do sit down." They both sat.

"So, how are things at Broad Oak?" asked Bethany, smiling.

"Brooksham," corrected the head teacher. Bethany face's flushed a shade of pink.

"Oh, I do beg your pardon, Mr Hartley, I'm jumping ahead of myself. I'm seeing Mr Sanders from Broad Oak immediately after you."

"I'm Mr Sanders," said Mr Sanders.

Bethany's face was now crimson as she asked, "From Broad Oak?"

"No, I'm head at Brooksham. Mr Hartley's head at Broad Oak."

Bethany was engulfed in total and acute embarrassment but tried to laugh it off.

"How silly of me," she said, "Mr *Sanders*, of course! You wouldn't believe I've got three degrees, now would you? I don't know what you must think. This is all a bit new to me."

"Not to worry, Ms Sedgeford," replied Mr Sanders. "It's easily done."

"Do call me Bethany, please. So, how are things at Brooksham?" she said with a forced laugh.

"All a bit difficult at the moment. We've just had the dreaded SATS tests and we had one of our Year Six teachers off throughout last term."

"I'm sure your results will be splendid."

"Well, we're hoping to be well above the national average again but you never can tell."

"No, you certainly can't. Now let me get straight to the point. I'm meeting all local primary heads at the moment because I think it's so very important to maintain close relationships. After all, your pupils are our future pupils and we ought to make sure that you are fully aware of the enormous benefits that these children will receive when they decide on this school as their first choice."

"Such as?"

"I'm sorry?" said Bethany, almost affronted.

"Oh, don't get me wrong, Ms Sedgeford. I'm sure there would be great benefits but how is your school any different from the several other good secondary schools in the catchment area? After all, your GCSE results are lagging behind."

"Under the previous head, yes," answered Southgreen's new Principal, by way of qualification, "but now we are one of the first schools with the new Academy status, I am making sweeping changes and I'm confident that these will be noticed and, indeed, praised in any forthcoming inspection. Anyway, results aren't everything. I'm sure you'd agree it's the quality of life in a school that's paramount and here at Southgreen Academy we try to produce rounded individuals who are polite, energetic and adaptable."

"Of course that's admirable but it still doesn't –"

But Bethany didn't want her flow interrupted. "Take the farm, for instance. How many other young students know what it's like to see animals being born and witness their development, while they care and tend to them from the cattle stall to the abattoir?"

"Yes, well of course the farm is a very strong point in favour," said Mr Sanders but Bethany stopped him again.

"It certainly is. None of the other schools provide such extensive rural studies in such enriching surroundings. It's our jewel in the crown, enhancing our community by providing all that's good about the traditions of rural life, as we say in our mission statement."

Just then, they heard a whining outside in the corridor. The door slowly opened and they became aware of the pointed tip of an orange traffic cone, which penetrated the space and then withdrew, accompanied by the sound of snivelling. Receding footsteps and a sudden howl were then heard as Ms Sedgeford rose from her chair and crossed to the door.

"Do excuse me for a moment, Mr Sanders."

She opened the door and, almost shouting, but still aware of her visitor's sensibilities, she said, "Peter Sutcliffe, what on earth have you got that ridiculous thing on your head for?" There was no response other than another bout of painful wailing. "I'm in a very important meeting, with a very important person and I can't deal with this now."

Peter then tried to yank the offending cone off, but without success, and this led to another agonising shriek. He then started wheezing and Bethany could see that he was also covered in grass. Bethany shouted her instructions. "Peter you need to go to the medical room to see the nurse and to have a puff on your inhaler." Peter was just about to speak when Bethany warned, "And now is not the appropriate time to bring up School Council business, as Mr Swinton told you not half an hour ago!" After these words Bethany was relieved to see Peter sloping off towards the medical room. She returned to her office.

"I'm most dreadfully sorry. Silly boy in year ten's got a traffic cone stuck to his head."

"Yes, I'd rather gathered," said the longsuffering Mr Sanders.

"The things they get up to," added Bethany.

"Indeed," said the primary head as Helga entered and placed a cup of percolated coffee in front of him.

"Thank you, Helga," said Bethany. "I thought I'd give you a guided tour, Mr Sanders. We'll start with the school farm."

♦ ♦ ♦

Dave was collating some photocopying when Sebastian entered the staff room. Simultaneously, the phone started ringing. He looked at Dave as if to say, "You were here first," but Dave gestured that his hands were full. Sebastian let out a huge sigh, just to rub in his annoyance and answered the phone.

"Yes! ... what? Well isn't there someone down there who can deal with it or do I have to do everything myself in this fucking place ... He's done what? You're kidding! That's all we fucking need to start the week. Does he know how much these things cost? I'll be straight down."

Sebastian turned to Dave, fuming. "That's what you get when you employ a fucking luvvie as a supply teacher!"

"What now?" asked Dave.

"There's a riot in Room 42 brought about by the supply, Mr Carter, deciding to use a bright red, fucking indelible board pen on the interactive whiteboard! That's fifteen hundred quid down the swanny; that is, if I can get down there before he does any more fucking damage!"

Sebastian's angry expression turned to one of delight when he saw the beautiful face of Françoise Poitin. Of course he knew she was thirty years younger than him and way out of his league but he never missed an opportunity to try to chat her up so, in his dreadful French accent he said, "Bonjour, Mademoiselle Poitin!"

"Bonjour Monsieur Swinton," came the response.

"Etes vous allez en France pendant les vacances?" said Sebastian.

"No, Basil. Oh, I hope you don't mind me calling you that –"

"No, no," said Sebastian, through gritted, English teeth.

"Everybody else does," continued Françoise. "Anyway, I stayed here for half term."

"No boyfriend to visit back in France then?" enquired Sebastian, hopefully.

"That's for me to know, Basil," said Françoise, playing along.

"Is it? Is it, indeed?" continued Sebastian before he was stopped in his tracks by Dave saying, "I thought there was a riot in Room 42?"

"Yes, alright, but it'll wait, it'll wait. Oh, I suppose I'd better ..." and with that Sebastian left, making exaggerated pointing gestures behind the French teacher's back, telling Dave, in no uncertain terms, that she was his, before Dave said, "Run along now, Basil," rubbing salt into the wound.

"Mr Swinton is so funny," said Françoise after he'd gone.

"If you like that sort of thing," said Dave. "He's an acquired taste."

"How do you mean?"

"Like cheap wine. Tastes like vinegar but if you drink enough of it you won't notice. Is it raining outside?"

"No, it's a beautiful day."

"It's just that your hair's wet."

"Yes, I washed it earlier."

"Oh," said Dave. He paused for a second and then said, "You're a bit keen aren't you?"

"I beg your pardon?"

"No, it's just that I saw your 2CV parked here at the end of half term."

"Oh, yes?"

"She's keen, I thought."

"No, it was just that I'd ... left some work here," replied a worried Françoise.

She had good cause to be, as Dave then said, "Thought it was your car. Can't mistake it with that stripy red, white and blue roof. Parked next to Andy's Audi."

"Andy?" said Françoise, playing dumb.

"You know, Andy Bailey. Head of PE."

"No, I don't think I've -"

"You mean you've been here a month and you don't know Andy?" said Dave.

"I probably do but I can't place him."

"He's slipping then," said Dave, enjoying this exchange now.

"Sorry?" said Françoise.

"Well it doesn't usually take long for Andy to start chatting up any pretty new teacher who arrives here," explained Dave.

"Really? Well, yes, he must be, how do you say, slipping?" said Françoise.

"Guess he'll get round to it eventually. Don't say I didn't warn you," said Dave.

"Thanks, I'll remember," said Françoise. And she would too.

♦ ♦ ♦

Long before Southgreen had become an academy it had boasted a school farm, which always had been and still was, as Bethany had told Mr Sanders, their jewel in the crown. In times past, many of the children had come from families that had a strong association with farming, their parents either being farm labourers or working in one of the chain of related industries, manufacturing farm tools and equipment or, indeed, selling, hiring and maintaining farm machinery, like tractors, ploughs and combine harvesters. Some of this was less so now, as there were fewer labourers needed, and tourism had grown, but this part of South East England had always been farming country and probably always would be.

Of course most of the large landowner farmers wouldn't let their children anywhere near Southgreen. They preferred to send them away to public school as boarders or to one of the many private schools in the near locality. There was also a private, independent school, very close by, that creamed off the best students from Southgreen at the age of thirteen. This had always been a problem, as it meant that the thirteen year olds that didn't get into the independent school were not the brightest academically. Consequently, the results had been on the slide and, in an education system that measured everything by exam results, this was a persistent difficulty. The worse the exam results got, the less likely parents were to choose Southgreen as the school for their children.

So, after the school had been forced into becoming one of the new academies, because of dreadful exam outcomes, Bethany Sedgeford had been appointed as the new Principal and her mission was to get results at whatever cost. As she'd said to Helga, it was a numbers game and she would use any means at her disposal to encourage both parents, as well as primary heads and teachers, to point children in the direction of Southgreen Academy. This was not going to be an easy task but she knew that the lure of the farm and the animals was the best hope they had, for both children and parents generally loved animals and it was something that none of the other local comprehensives could boast.

So, as Bethany stood beside the tall figure of Mr Sanders, she looked up to him as the first head teacher that she might be able to impress and, despite her shaky start, neither knowing his name nor the school that he represented, she was going to make amends.

Things didn't begin however quite as smoothly as she would have liked. As they walked across the field, Bethany was explaining farm matters to him.

"Of course the Herefords over there make up the bulk of our cattle herd. They're mainly grass fed and the meat is top quality. Are you a meat eater, Mr Sanders?"

"Yes, for my sins," he replied.

"The Jersey herd are primarily for milking. I'll show you them when we get to the milking stalls, next to the piggery."

Just then Mr Sanders noticed that the Herefords, who were in the corner of the field, were slowly walking towards them, led by the largest animal, who seemed to be fixing him with a stare.

"They seem to be following us, Ms Sedgeford," said Mr Sanders, appearing a little agitated.

"They're only being friendly," said Bethany, reassuringly. "Whatever you do, don't run, just walk steadily towards the gate."

But Mr Sanders wasn't sure that this was good advice, as the cattle were now moving faster, indeed had they been horses he would have said they were trotting. He began to walk faster too and so did Bethany. "Remember, don't run, just walk quickly," repeated Bethany but when Mr Sanders turned again he was even more alarmed as the cattle were now cantering towards them and some were mooing their disapproval at the intruders, whom Mr Sanders was quickly realising were Ms Sedgeford and his good self! He started to stretch his long legs faster and so did Bethany, who continued with her previous advice saying, "Don't run, Mr Sanders," but then she turned and saw the cattle getting very close now and almost stampeding, so she cried out, more through self-preservation than anything else, "Run, Mr Sanders. Run!" And run they both did but, after a few strides, Mr Sanders' shoe came off and he stopped to pick it up, with the leader of the herd bearing down on him. Bethany got ahead, reaching the iron gate and clambering over. She then turned to see Mr Sanders being forced to leap, encouraged by a large bovine mouth mooing to his rear. Mr Sanders had always considered being tall an advantage, as he could tower over others at crowded events, getting the best view but, just at this moment, it was a complete liability for, as he jumped and landed astride the top bar of the iron gate, his shoeless foot touched the electric fence, sitting at right angles and adjacent to the gate and the high voltage shot up his leg and surged through his precariously balanced crotch. He gave out a yelp of pain, as the shock of electricity coursing through his testicles, catapulted him over the gate, where he landed in an ignominious heap, clutching his crotch, at the entrance to the field, with the entire herd of Hereford's, staring through the bars of the gate, silently ruminating on his misfortune.

It was therefore, something of a relief when, after picking himself up and accepting Ms Sedgeford's fulsome apology, they both arrived at the farm buildings.

They were greeted by Mr Bull, who Bethany introduced to the unfortunate Mr Sanders. Brian was feeding a small piglet from a bottle, cradling it in his arms as carefully as he would his own child.

"What happened to its mother?" asked Mr Sanders, brushing the mud off his trousers and stepping from foot to foot to ease the pain.

"Anne Widdecombe?" said Brian.

"Sorry?" said Mr Sanders.

"His mum; named after Anne Widdecombe. We call her Annie for short and she's our prize winning sow, but she's got enough on her plate with eight other piglets gnawing away at her teats. This is Boris, the runt of the litter."

"Mr Bull has a curious method of naming the pigs, Mr Sanders. He names the sows after famous, celebrity, fat women, all of them extremely talented, many being national treasures but also known for helping the great British public in the war against obesity. And the young boars he names alphabetically. Not very politically correct, I know, but the animals don't seem to mind."

Mr Bull explained more fully, while little Boris suckled on the teat of the bottle, which was rapidly emptying. "Boris was her ninth and last. We've got Jo Brand due soon and her first boar will be called Christopher or Calum or Charles, or some such, unless Vanessa Feltz beats her to it, in which case Jo Brand will have to be content with a Dennis or a Derek or a Dinsdale."

"What other animals do you have?" asked Mr Sanders.

"Cows, sheep, goats, the usual," said Mr Bull, "as well as chickens, ducks, geese, rabbits and, of course, our prize winning turkeys."

"You forgot Casanova," said Bethany, helpfully.

"Oh, yes, our champion pet ram. He gets all the fun. You'll see him in a minute and I use the term 'pet' advisedly as you definitely don't want him coming up behind you."

"Do you have any bulls?" asked Mr Sanders, rather in trepidation because, after his recent experience with the cattle, he certainly didn't want to meet one.

"No." said Brian. "The cows are all artificially inseminated and it's an integral and natural part of GCSE coursework for all Rural Science students to witness our vet, young Mr McGregor, donning his long rubber glove and doing the business. Some of the cows can't get up that ramp fast enough into the holding stall."

"You mean?"

"Yes, Mr Sanders, he gives the girls a treat, slides his whole arm in with the syringe, squirts up the semen and it's over in a flash!"

Laughing loudly, Bethany added, "Not very different to human beings, eh, Mr Sanders," whose face flushed with embarrassment. "Oh, I'm terribly sorry, I don't know what you must think of me. The farm brings us all down to earth and it also has wonderful cross curricular possibilities: Biology, Rural Science and Sex Education all rolled into one. The students love it!"

"I'm sure they do," said Mr Sanders.

"If you don't mind me asking, Mr Sanders, what do you and your family like to eat at Christmas?"

"Well, we had a goose last year, for a change, but my children weren't that impressed, so I've promised them a turkey next time."

"Yes, children can be so conservative can't they?" said Bethany. "I only ask because there's always the possibility of a Christmas hamper coming your way. How are we fixed for turkeys this year, Mr Bull?"

"Oh, I think a turkey could be arranged. Possibly a leg of lamb too, a loin of pork, a side of beef even, depending on the numbers," said Brian.

"Sorry, I don't quite understand," said Mr Sanders.

"What Mr Bull is getting at," explained Bethany, "is that here at Southgreen, we think it only right that we reward local heads who convey to parents the educational benefits of choosing our school first for Secondary Education."

Now, getting it absolutely, Mr Sanders said, "Are you trying to bribe me, Ms Sedgeford?"

"Certainly not!" Bethany shot back, "and it offends me to think you could possibly think such a thing. It's purely a little thank you to those heads that see the advantages of Southgreen Academy's unique way of preparing students for the hostility of the outside world. Think of it more as an incentive. How many other local comprehensives can show off a fully working agricultural establishment. I'll tell you, Mr Sanders, none. None! You're not telling me you're not impressed?"

"No, really, I am, I think it's marvellous. I didn't mean to offend you."

Just then, the sound of Pachelbel's Canon could be heard coming from the milking stalls.

"What's that?" asked Mr Sanders.

"Classical music. It relaxes the cows and increases the milk yield," said Mr Bull. "Though I find they like a bit of modern stuff too. Here, have a hold of Boris." Mr Bull passed the little piglet over to Mr Sanders for him to hold, then gave him a fresh bottle saying, "Give him another one. He's a greedy guts, is Boris."

Immediately, Mr Sanders was won over. He whispered, "Hello, little Boris, hello," as he started to feed him the bottle. Then he turned to Bethany and said, "Isn't he lovely?"

"Indeed he is, Mr Sanders, indeed he is."

"You're a natural," said Mr Bull. "A dead ringer for old Anne Widdecombe ... and Boris has definitely taken a shine to you."

Bethany smiled at Brian, in acknowledgement of a good job done, while the strains of Pachelbel's Canon faded. The cows however continued to be calmed by the next track on the compilation CD, as George Harrison's scouse vocal about piggies could be heard, emanating from the speakers above the milking stalls.

♦ ♦ ♦

The staffroom clock read 09.55 and it had already been an eventful day in the life of young Tom Carter, who was now facing the most vicious haranguing from the apoplectic Vice Principal.

"What in the name of God did you think you were doing, Mr Carter?"

"I'm sorry, Mr Swinton, really, I just didn't realise," said Tom, guiltily.

"Didn't realise? Didn't fucking realise! Didn't they teach you anything at college?" Sebastian asked, trying not to raise his voice too loudly, in fear of the boss hearing his anger fuelled expletives.

Tom's not unreasonable excuse was, "I studied Drama and, anyway, interactive whiteboards hadn't come in then, so I wasn't trained for -"

"But it's fucking obvious!" exclaimed Sebastian. "What induced you to scrawl all over it in fucking, bright red, indelible board pen? I mean do you realise how much fucking money these things cost? It's fifteen hundred nicker down the toilet, Mr Carter, all because of you!"

"I'm really sorry, Mr Swinton. I asked the students what to do and one of them gave me the pen and said I should just write with it."

"Well of course they fucking did you idiot! They're children for Christ's sake. You don't think these lowest math's set, Year 10 bastards come to school to learn do you? They come to wind us up and have a fucking good laugh at our expense!"

Tom continued, "Then another one said that I'd used the wrong pen and it was indelible and the only way I could get it off was to spray this cleaning stuff on, so I did and then I rubbed it with a cloth and that only made things worse!"

"If I could take it out of your wages I would. What's your daily rate?"

"About a hundred and ten pounds."

"Plus the fucking agency fee. Well Mr Paedophile, luvvie Carter, that's the best part of seventeen hundred quid you've cost us and look at the time - oh, how it just flies when you're enjoying yourself - it's only fucking ten o'clock!"

Tom was saved anymore humiliation by the sound of the bell and Dave Hardman's appearance.

"If it isn't bleeding Davy Crocket," said Sebastian. "Seriously, Dave, thanks for holding the fort. Any joy?"

"Mr Doyle's in the process of dismantling the board."

"Is he indeed. Dismantling seems to be Mr Doyle's *principal* word of the day. See, Mr Carter, stupidity always has its repercussions. I'm sure Mr Doyle had far more important things to do than to clear up your fucking disaster area." With that, Sebastian left and Dave tried to ease Tom's conscience, saying, "I wouldn't worry too much. It's an easy mistake to make if you don't know."

"I just didn't think."

"Oh, you don't need to think here. This is a school, after all. I wouldn't worry; it'll be covered on the insurance."

"That's a bit of a relief," said Tom. "I've got 10JD next. What are they like?"

"Unpredictable. There's a big lad in there called, Carl Borman, that they're all terrified of, only they hate him even more. Put him in detention straight away and you won't have any trouble from the others."

Dave pulled off a wad of referral forms, as Tom asked, "But what if he doesn't do anything wrong?"

"Oh, he will do, don't you worry. If, on the slim chance he doesn't, provoke him by saying you support Spurs, because he's a fanatical Arsenal fan; that should do the trick."

Dave gave Tom the forms, saying, "Tick the relevant boxes. Put one copy in his mentor's pigeon hole and the other in Seb's. You'd better go. Tell you what; if I don't see you at break and you fancy a lunchtime pint, I'll be off down the Royal Oak at 12.20 sharp. You can fill me in on your illustrious career."

As Tom hurried down the corridor, to his next lesson, he had no idea that the terrible start he'd had at Southgreen Academy was only going to get worse and that Carl Borman was a name that, in the course of the next few weeks, would give him nightmares.

♦ ♦ ♦

The clock in the staff room read 10.40 as the room began to fill for break. The support staff were gossiping quietly, until Susan Shepherd, dropped a cream cake all over another teaching assistant, making a terrible mess and causing more activity than usual from their direction.

Mr Hill must have been awake at some point, as he had a full cup of espresso, precariously balanced on the arm of his chair and he was clinging on to a half-eaten packet of Cheeselets, but now he was definitely in a state of cataplexy though, if someone had put a mirror to his lips, it would have shown that he was still, almost certainly, breathing.

Sebastian was telling Dave about Mr Carter's difficult second lesson. Tom knew they were talking about him, even though he was drinking coffee alone, sat on the other side of the staff room. The body language said it all.

"I just don't know where these agencies find these people, Dave, I really don't. Carl Borman was literally foaming at the mouth by the time I arrived. He was giving our young paedophile, Mr Carter over there the Nazi salute and goose stepping round the classroom. Then he started shouting anti-Semitic, racist abuse at him and finally turned on me, calling me 'another fucking yid.' So, it's another exclusion till the end of the week which is, at least, something to be thankful for. Wish I could pack him off to Argentina."

Exuding guilt, Dave said, "I think that might have been down to me," as he crossed to speak to Tom.

"I owe you an apology," said Dave.

"I did exactly as you told me," said Tom.

"And?"

"Well, he was good as gold to begin with, sitting right in front of me, so I said, quite casually, 'did you see Thierry Henry miss that sitter last night?' So, he goes absolutely berserk and starts saying that I'm racist and that I'm only having a go at Henry because he's black and that he's the best player and Arsenal are the best team in the world and, anyway, who did I fucking support? So I put him in detention for swearing and he repeated the question and I said, 'Spurs' and he just goes completely ape shit and starts calling me 'a fucking yid' and doing the Nazi salute and saying Hitler had the right idea and that he would personally build his own gas chamber and incinerate all Spurs fans."

"Carl Borman used the word incinerate?" asked Dave.

"Yes," said Tom.

"I'm impressed."

Tom continued, "And I'd had enough by now because, contrary to what you had told me, all the others were egging him on, so I said it was a bit rich him calling me a racist after what he'd just said, and did he know that Hitler's chief henchman was called 'Borman' too, to which he replied that he fucking did, but it was spelt differently, that he wasn't fucking thick, and that he quite frequently watched programmes about the Nazis, on the History Channel, till two o'clock in the morning!"

Contrite, Dave said, "What was it Seb said before about stupidity always having its repercussions? I'm sorry, it's entirely my fault for giving you such stupid advice. The first round is on me."

Others were chatting in pairs and small groups. Dick was with Randy Andy.

"French after break, then?"

"No, I'm free," replied Andy.

"But I thought you were brushing up on your French in your office," said Dick.

"Yeah, I was," replied Andy, "but Basil changed the cover, so there was no need."

Helga, crossing to the photocopier, heard Mr Dylan offering Françoise a chocolate éclair. She was just about to take one from the packet when Helga said, "Oh, I wouldn't touch them. They're well past their sell by date. They've been in the fridge since before half term." She then relieved Mr Dylan of the offending package.

Dick was watching and whispered to Andy, "I bet that Françoise bird's a bit of a goer."

"Doesn't do it for me," replied Andy.

"Well, Mr Tambourine Man seems to be launching the old charm offensive."

"You must be joking," said Andy. "Our Mr Dylan over there's got about as much charm as a cup of cold sick. All he ever talks about is whether he's going to get Hilly Billy's job when he retires. I bet you a Kit Kat that's what he's saying to her right now."

"Never," said Dick. "I'll raise you a Penguin, he's chatting her up."

Dick and Andy sidled over towards Mr Dylan and Françoise, who said, "I can see it must be very frustrating not knowing what the outcome will be."

"Well, I've been here nine years," said Mr Dylan "and it's not as though Southgreen was my first school. I've been second in the department for six, so it really should be mine by rights."

Francoise qualified this with, "They have to advertise though, don't they?"

"Yes, that's the point, see. It's a legal requirement."

Andy pumped the air and Dick looked crestfallen. He was number two to Andy, not only in the PE department hierarchy but also in everything else they did. Andy always won at games and, of course, gained the attention of the young women in the school. Now he'd won some chocolate. But Mr Dylan hadn't finished.

"I mean, to be honest, I've been doing his job more or less for the last two years, the amount of time he's had off with his sleeping sickness." Andy was now behind Mr Dylan making yawning gestures directed towards Françoise, who was having difficulty keeping a straight face. Mr Dylan, oblivious to Andy's antics, continued, "Of course the boss has said some very ambiguous things but I don't know if she's winding me up, see."

Now, Andy was leaning behind Dick and pretending to sniff his armpits, then waving his hands to dissipate the imaginary smell, with a look of disgust.

Mr Dylan finished the conversation and finally settled Dick and Andy's bet, saying, "I didn't need to have been here all this time. If I'd been like some of the others, I could have upped sticks and got a Head of Department job years ago."

With this Andy whispered to Dick, "That's one Kit Kat and a Penguin you owe me." Now it was time for him to wind Mr Dylan up.

"Have they fixed a date for the interviews yet?"

"No," said Mr Dylan, "it's imminent, I'm told."

"Well, with so many people applying I suppose it takes time to organise."

This worried Mr Dylan. "So many?"

"Record numbers, I'm informed."

"Really?"

"Yes, well it stands to reason doesn't it? Plumb job in the South East. There must be scientists queuing up for that kind of opportunity. Some of these Oxbridge graduates; I mean all they need to do now is take the 'golden hello,' do a year or two in one school and then, speed of light, they're head of department."

Françoise was angered. Liberté, égalité, fraternité was etched onto her psyche.

"Yes, it's so unfair, the old boy network. Isn't that how you say it?"

"Got it in one," said Mr Dylan. "We should have done what your lot did and guillotined the bastards!"

Andy warned Mr Tambourine Man off. "Steady, Mr Dylan. If the boss gets wind you're a revolutionary you'll be shovelling pig shit before old Hilly Billy retires."

Just then Sebastian entered the room and made a beeline for Françoise.

"My dear Mademoiselle Poitin," said Sebastian, "or dare I call you ma cherie?" Receiving no affirmation, he continued, "I hate to break up your scintillating break time conversation with these three, testosterone pumping, primates here but I'd just like to inform you that Peter Sutcliffe is waiting in the corridor and craves your undivided attention."

"But I don't teach Peter Sutcliffe," said Françoise.

Sebastian continued, "Be that as it may, Mademoiselle, Peter has this rather unappealing habit of hammering away until he gets his way with whoever it may be and, though I have told him quite forcefully to bugger off, he is now been reduced to tears because the nurse has just removed a rather large traffic cone from his head, and he's insisting that he needs to talk to you about something extremely important." Françoise, who had become a teacher for the noble reason of genuinely wanting to help improve the lives of young people and encourage them in every sense said, "Well I don't mind; if he's that concerned." She left the room quickly and consequently didn't hear Sebastian say, "Don't say you haven't been warned."

Over near Mr Hill, Dave and Tom were chatting. Tom couldn't help be fascinated by the sight of the elderly teacher, fast asleep in his chair.

"He doesn't have much to say for himself," he said.

"No," said Dave, "the battle was beyond him in the end."

"How do you mean?"

"Well, I don't say this lightly because 'there but for the grace' and all that, but he's become completely institutionalised. He gave in years ago and school life now washes over him like the idiomatic dullness of ditch water. He could have retired over ten years ago but he's one of the old school who just had to battle on till the bitter end and beyond. He's seen all the changes over the last forty years and, believe you me, none of them have made the slightest difference to him. I bet he's going about his teaching much as he did in the 1960s, except now he's got a laptop and about one percent of the enthusiasm and idealism that he had when he started. That's all been knocked out of him through years of political neglect. He's been swamped by endless directives from bureaucrats and bullied into submission by management until, for a time, he became a bully himself; it was the only way to survive. But now he's jumped through so many hoops that he's spiralling down a black hole, completely tired out and disappearing into the immensely dense singularity of nothing."

Tom and Dave looked at Mr Hill in unison and his motionless hand suddenly moved, as if by reflex action and knocked the cup of espresso, balanced on the arm of his chair, off and down onto the floor. It shattered, hitting the base of the chair leg where Tom was sitting. Mr Hill didn't wake. Tom and Dave looked at each other. They both thought the same thought. Somehow this was a significant moment in their lives. They both started to pick up the broken pieces of china as Françoise returned, holding a piece of paper.

Sebastian asked, "Well, what did the young Sutcliffe have to say for himself then?"

After a beat, Françoise said, "He's written me a poem."

"Stone me," said Sebastian, "what will he think of next? Well, aren't you going to read it to us then, give us all a laugh?"

"No, it's private," said Françoise, firmly. She started to read the poem to herself but then stopped, saying, "No, I will read it, I will. It's good. Listen."

A hush had descended on the staff room as, suddenly, everybody became interested. Françoise started to read Peter's poem.

> "My eye has played the painter and has drawn
> Your beauty's form, a picture from my heart.
> My body is the frame in which it's born,
> Perspective is the summit of my art.
> For through the painter you will see his skill,
> And find where your true image copied lies.
> It hangs in my heart's gallery and still,
> Has windows gleaming now through your bright eyes.
> Now view the good exchanging eyes have done:
> My eyes have drawn your shape and yours for me
> Are portholes to my heart, through which the sun
> Delights to spy my mermaid out at sea.
> Yet clever eyes still lack the perfect art,
> Draw just the vision yet don't touch the heart."

Françoise folded the paper and the silence was only disturbed by Sebastian, saying, completely inappropriately, "Well, bugger me sideways, Peter Sutcliffe wrote that?"

Helga wiped away a tear saying, "It's beautiful," while Susan Shepherd started blubbing and had to be given a tissue by a colleague.

"He's drawn a beautiful picture of me too," said Françoise.

Sebastian was both surprised and impressed and said, "Who would have thought that that spotty, ginger nerd, who drives us all to distraction, could have written something as poetic as that?"

"It's not original, of course," said Dave.

"Not original? Not original?" said Sebastian in disbelief. "It's better than some of the crap that passes for poetry these days. I mean none of it rhymes or scans anymore and the more obscure it is the better. Give me 'a host of golden daffodils' any day of the week."

"It's Shakespeare for the most part; Sonnet twenty four," said Dave.

Cottoning on, Sebastian then showed his true colours. "You mean ...? I might have fucking guessed. Too clever for his own good is the slapper obsessed Sutcliffe but he can't pull the wool over the literary genius we have as Head of Southgreen's English department. Well done, Dave, of course it's Shakespeare. You should be on fucking Mastermind mate!"

"Give it a rest, Basil," said Dave.

"Sorry?" said Sebastian, annoyed at the sound of his nickname being used so blatantly.

"I wish you were," said Dave. "I set Peter the task."

"You mean?"

"In fact, I asked my best year 10 GCSE students to try to re-write Sonnet twenty four, preserving the meaning and removing as much archaic language as possible. Peter's effort was streets ahead of the rest. I particularly liked the way he changed windows to portholes and introduced the image of the mermaid out at sea. I think Shakespeare would have liked that too. He's A star material is our young Peter, even if he is a ginger nerd, as you say."

As the bell rang and the staff began to disperse, Dave crossed to the phone and dialled. Susan Shepherd, approached Dave, as if about to say something, but could do nothing more than wipe away more tears and blow her nose noisily into the tissue she was clutching.

"Hello," said Dave, "is that the National Theatre? ... Yes, you can. I'm calling to enquire about tickets for ' 'Tis Pity She's a Whore' ... Yes, that's right. It's in relation to your special discount scheme for students."

♦ ♦ ♦

Ms Bethany Sedgeford was pleased with the outcome, if not the experience of being chased by a herd of Herefords across a field and the unfortunate coming together of Mr Sander's testicles, the iron gate and an electric fence. The two subsequent visiting heads had found the story amusing (Bethany thought so too, delighting in the telling of it) but needed to get away quickly. They hadn't had a tour of the farm but Mr Amyes, Head of Bidhurst Primary, was now surveying the farm buildings again, holding forth, with her and Brian Bull his attentive audience.

"It's a lovely view from here across to Chapel Bank, isn't it, Mr Bull?" said Mr Amyes.

"Beautiful," said Brian.

Mr Amyes continued, "Amazing to think they dismantled the old church up there, stone by stone and moved it."

"When was that?" asked Bethany who, despite her lofty position, was no local.

"A bit before our time," said Mr Amyes. "Sixteenth Century. There were outbreaks of malaria in those days. The mosquitoes killed people, so they moved the church."

"You're a veritable fountain of knowledge, Mr Amyes," said Bethany.

"Do call me Silas, please. Yes, I was born not a stone's throw from Chapel Bank. Of course, I've seen some changes over the years but, by and large, we haven't done too badly. It's still such a lovely part of the world. Your students are very fortunate to have the benefits of this wonderful farm, Bethany. Mr Bull here does a brilliant job."

Bethany replied, "You don't have to tell me that," with a beaming smile, as broad as the prize sow, Annie's bottom. "I can see I don't have to do much persuading with you to justify the merits of Southgreen over our competitors. Play your cards right, Silas and, with sufficient numbers, there might be a Christmas hamper coming your way. How are we fixed for turkeys this year, Mr Bull?"

Well primed now, Brian replied, "Oh, I think a turkey could be arranged. Possibly a leg of lamb too; a loin of pork; a side of beef even, depending on the –"

Mr Amyes butted in, "Are you two trying to bribe me?"

"Certainly not! And it offends me to think you could possibly say such a –"

But butting in again, like the champion ram Casanova, Mr Amyes said, "Hold your horses. Don't go all moralistic on me, Bethany. Did I say I wasn't up for a good old fashioned perk? I can assure you that the vast majority of Bidhurst Primary will be wearing the Southgreen uniform by September. And, as for the hamper, all the things you said, thank you Brian, plus a goose wouldn't go amiss, as we've got the in laws over from the states this Christmas."

"I think that can be arranged, eh Ms Sedgeford?"

"Indeed it can, Brian, and indeed it will," said Bethany, now revelling in her public relations triumph but, just at that moment,

Mr Bull's mobile phone sounded with a ringtone that played the first bars of 'Old McDonald had a farm.'

"Excuse me a moment. Hello … you're joking … that was quick … boars you say … okay, I'll be right there. Would you credit it," he said to the others, "Vanessa Feltz has started!"

"You mean, she's having piglets right now?"

"Yes, Ms Sedgeford," said Brian, "she's already had two while we've been up here, both boys and I shall name them Calum and Dinsdale. So, Jo Brand will have to make do with an Eric or an Ernie, unless of course darling Vanessa has any more young boars."

Silas Amyes look bewildered, not being privy to Brian's peculiar method of naming the pigs.

"That was quick," said Bethany.

"I know," said Brian. "She was eating from the trough not half an hour ago. But a sow of Vanessa's experience has no trouble. See with pigs it's real natural childbirth; none of your gas and air and epidurals and all that malarkey. No, if Vanessa has a birth plan it's to squeeze 'em out, like so many squirts of toothpaste and get back to scoffing swill before you can say pork chops. "

"Shall we wander?" suggested Bethany.

"If you don't mind, I'll dash on ahead. The next little sow will be named Dawn, after the delectable Dawn French."

♦ ♦ ♦

Although drinking alcohol during the teaching day would have been frowned upon by the new Principal, old habits died hard at Southgreen. It had always given Dave something to look forward to, during the long mornings, and so a pint at the Royal Oak was a pre-requisite for him having a tolerable afternoon. He didn't mean to lead the young Tom Carter astray, nevertheless, he was itching to hear how Tom had got on after break and said, "No more disasters periods three and four?"

"Just the one," said Tom.

In a cod actor's deep tone, Dave replied, "Illuminate me, dear boy."

Tom did. "Period four and this kid was being really disruptive for the first five minutes, while I was explaining the work to the class. So, I give him the beady eye and warn him and then he drops his pencil tin, on purpose, and it crashes all over the floor. And now there are one or two others getting involved, you know how it is, picking up compasses and rulers and dropping them again, so I say to the boy, 'What's your name' and he goes, 'John Smith' and I scream at him, 'right that's a detention for you for being insolent!' And –"

"You don't have to tell me," said Dave, "his name *is* John Smith. 8RH. He does that with every teacher, the first time they teach him. It's a brilliant strategy. You see, John is always a bloody pain in the arse but, after he's set teachers up like that, they find it difficult being harsh with him in the future. It's the classic guilt trip and it works."

"Yes, I can see," said Tom. "It's not been my lucky day."

"That's an understatement, if ever I heard one, but don't let it get to you; you've got the whole of the afternoon to get through yet! Cheers," said Dave, raising his pint.

"Oh, yes, cheers," and they clinked glasses.

"So, what other things have you done then, apart from playing a paedophile in 'The Bill'?"

"Oh, quite a lot of stuff really," said Tom proudly, "considering I've only been out of college two years. Theatre, tele, radio."

"I'd love to be able to do that; get up on stage and perform. It must be exciting."

"Yes, it is, if you're in something that's really good, it can be a wonderful experience, a real buzz but -"

"If it's crap, it's the opposite?"

"Exactly."

"So, what's the crappiest thing you've ever done?"

"Well, I once played a nine foot penis at the Edinburgh Festival."

Dave nearly did the nose trick, almost spitting and snorting out his bitter as he laughed, but managed to ask, "In?"

"A terrible student piece about female exploitation and pornography, with the unlikely title, 'Up and Coming-Down and Out.' I was the token male but I had a lovely costume!"

Dave laughed even louder and said, "You get all the best parts." Talking of nine foot pricks, you should see our head of PE in operation."

"Really?"

"Yes, in fact, if it wasn't for Andy you wouldn't be here."

"How do you mean?"

"Well you're covering the Head of Maths, who's off sick with depression because she found out that Andy was shagging her at the same time as the student PE teacher. But, entre nous, he's shagging the new French teacher as well!"

"The one that read the poem?"

"Yes, Françoise," said Dave.

"She seems very nice," said Tom.

"Yes, she is. Sensitive, I'd say. Too good for Randy Andy."

"Françoise, you say?"

But Dave warned, "Now, don't go getting ideas or you'll have Andy to contend with and he's been known to turn nasty, has Andy. Anyway, I thought all actors were gay?"

♦ ♦ ♦

It was always around mid-afternoon that Bethany would get peckish and Helga knew this. Having just finished taking some letters in shorthand, she entered Bethany's office and placed a plate in front of her saying, "Would you like a chocolate éclair?"

"I shouldn't."

"Oh, go on," said Helga, encouraging her. "You know you want one really."

"You've twisted my arm," said Bethany, "but I'm supposed to be on a diet. If I eat too many of these, Mr Bull will be naming the next sow born after me!"

"Oh, I don't think so."

"I'm not being serious, Helga."

But Helga didn't care. "No, Brian only names the young sows after *famous fat* women. While you might be a woman you're definitely not famous and you're not fat either ... well not that fat!"

"Not yet, anyway," replied Bethany "and thank you for being so forthright, Helga, though you'd be surprised how far my reputation stretches. Had you forgotten that I'm also a Justice of the Peace? Now, I'm expecting Mr Dylan at any moment; just give me five minutes to tuck into this before you send him in."

"Very well," said Helga, reverting to her former subservience, but wryly smiling and revelling in her, about to be revealed, wickedness. For, as Helga left through the door to her part of the office, on the way to the staff room, Bethany picked up a copy of 'Hello' Magazine and eyed the chocolate éclair. She could not resist the enticement of the large dollop of cream, hanging on the end of the said bakery, so she licked it and then felt a little unsure.

But Helga didn't and caught an eager Mr Dylan just outside the door to the staff room.

"Is the boss in?" he said.

"Yes, go straight through, Mr Dylan, she's expecting you."

Following the School Secretary's instructions, the unsuspecting Mr Dylan crossed through Helga's part of the office and straight through the door into the Principal's office, without knocking, just as his superior had overcome her caution and was now taking an enormous bite from the rancid chocolate éclair.

"Helga said to come straight through, boss," said Mr Dylan, as Bethany recoiled from both the pastry, which (if only she'd known) was riddled with mould inside and the cream, which was off, and started retching, grabbing the wastepaper bin in a reflex reaction and coughing, before spitting out a large piece of bad, and now half chewed, chocolate éclair. A tiny piece of pastry covered in sickly, sour cream remained and tasted disgusting, so Bethany started retching again immediately, looking as if she was choking and Mr Dylan rushed across and grabbed her by the waste from behind.

"No, please," Bethany tried to say but couldn't.

"Don't worry," said Mr Dylan, reassuringly but at the same time, thinking about his promotion, "I'm going to perform the Heimlich Manoeuvre. I'm a trained first aider."

Coughing and spluttering, Bethany managed to blurt out, incoherently, "You don't need to do that. It was only a chocolate éclair," but Mr Dylan had already wrapped his arms around her, clasping his hands firmly together, just beneath her solar plexus, and then started exerting severe pressure, jerking his hands and Bethany backwards. She tried to get him to stop, but couldn't get the words out and just let out a long moaning sound, as the door to the office opened, revealing an astonished Helga. "I'm terribly sorry, I should have knocked," she said and left immediately. Bethany managed to recover enough to exclaim, "Stop!" and Mr Dylan finally released his grasp saying,

"Something must have gone down the wrong way."

Bethany put him right however saying, "I wasn't choking. It was the chocolate éclair. The cream's off!"

"I could've told you that," said the heroic Welsh first aider. "They've been in the fridge since before half term; Helga told us not to touch them at break."

"Did she? Did she, indeed?" said Bethany, her suspicions now aroused.

"I'm sorry boss, I thought you were choking."

"It's quite alright. Thank you, Mr Dylan. I know you were only trying to help."

As he breathed an audible sigh of relief, Helga could almost hear it, holding her ear pressed to the other side of the door. But she couldn't hear the Principal as she lowered her voice and said, "I've been having my doubts about Helga."

"She was very attached to old Mr Foulkes," said Mr Dylan.

"Yes, I know she was," replied Bethany, quietly. "What must have she been thinking?"

She got up from her kneeling position and held her fingers to her lips, by way of instruction to the Deputy Head of Science. She approached the door, not making a sound but Helga had a sixth sense and, just as Bethany opened the door sharply, she moved away, pretending to write on her note pad.

"Mr Harris, the Chief Inspector has just called. He says can you ring him back ASAP."

Mr Dylan appeared at Bethany's shoulder saying, "I think the boss could do with a drink of water, Helga."

"Well, I think a cigarette is customary in this situation."

"I was choking, Helga. Mr Dylan here had to perform the Heimlich Manoeuvre," said Bethany.

"Of course he did," replied Helga. "I could see. He seemed to be enjoying himself too!"

"Don't be ridiculous, really! It wasn't what it must have looked like," said the unusually, flustered Principal.

Enjoying this now, Helga replied, "Don't worry, my lips are sealed."

But Bethany doubted that they were, as Helga left and made her way to the staff room.

Bethany beckoned Mr Dylan back into her office and closed the door.

"I can't imagine why she would have done such a thing?"

"Maybe she made a mistake," replied the Welshman. "Maybe they weren't the same éclairs as this morning."

"There's only one way to find out. Mr Dylan, you know how much I value loyalty?"

"Absolutely, boss," said Mr Dylan, who would now do anything at all to impress his employer.

"Would you mind?"

"Mind, boss?"

"Popping to the staff room and finding the packet. Checking the sell by date for me? It's probably in the bin."

"Oh, well ... yes, of course I don't mind."

"Off you pop, then," said Bethany. So Mr Dylan did pop off and found Helga at the photocopier, as he entered the staff room.

"You're a dark horse," she said.

"Don't be daft, Helga. I told you already, I was performing the Heimlich Manoeuvre. I thought she was choking."

"I bet that's not the only manoeuvring you're up to," said Helga, now relishing her new, powerful status, after what she had witnessed.

"What do you mean?" asked the worried man.

"Oh, not much gets past me, Mr Dylan. You should know that by now," said Helga, noticing the Welsh life saver dithering about in the kitchen area.

"Looking for something?" she asked.

"Oh, yes, my mug."

"Behind you on the hooks," said Helga, helpfully. "Where they've been for the last ten years. I think yours is the one that says, 'GENIUS' in large, black letters."

Mr Dylan was fed up with Helga now, as she was preventing him from the task it was so very necessary for him to undertake. After all, promotion could depend on it.

"Oh, I just remembered," he said. "Mr Doyle was looking for you before; said it was really urgent."

"Yes, well he'll just have to wait," said Helga. "It's probably about the adult learning course that Ms Sedgeford has insisted he sign up for, after the dressing down he got about his spelling this morning." She picked up her photocopying and returned to her office.

Thinking he was safe, Mr Dylan started to rummage through the contents of a rather smelly bin but was stopped in his tracks and shuffled away, pretending to make coffee, as Helga returned. She crossed to the photocopier and lifted the top cover to collect the original document that she had left behind. Then she went back to her office.

The coast now clear, Mr Dylan returned to the bin and, digging down, located the offending chocolate éclair package, looking at the date on the label and checking to see if there were any others. He glanced at his watch and then started to count back on his fingers. He got to ten and smiled with the knowledge that he was about to confirm the Principal's worst fears.

♦ ♦ ♦

The staff room clock now read 15.40 as Sebastian, Tom, Dave and Françoise all entered together.

"So, Mr luvvie dovey Carter, you're in business," said Sebastian as Bethany approached from her office.

"All okay with the buses, Seb?" she asked.

"Oh, yes boss, just the one member of staff carted off to casualty today," he replied.

"No," said Bethany. "Who and why?"

"Well, one extremely irresponsible and impatient parent broke all the rules, blocked off two coaches in the parking area and then, reacting to me waving them frantically away, managed to reverse over the unfortunate teacher's foot. Luckily, it was Mr Wiseman, our drama teacher and, as fate would have it, we have the perfect replacement here in our young luvvie, Mr Carter, who has had, shall we say, a trying, not to say expensive day in the maths department. Needless to say, boss, I've immediately booked another supply to replace our depressed Head of Maths, who happens to actually be, oh miracle of miracles, a fully qualified teacher of mathematics. Which only goes to prove that, just once in a while, E does indeed equal MC squared!"

"And how is Mr Wiseman's foot?" asked Bethany.

"Still attached to his leg when last seen, boss," said Sebastian, "but he's definitely not going to make it in for a day or two, so we'll just have to wait on the medics."

"Right, Seb, I'm just going to powder my nose and we'll start the meeting."

◆ ◆ ◆

The support staff hated after school meetings. Officially, they didn't have to attend, as they weren't paid to do so, but it was frowned upon if they didn't and they knew that, if they stayed away, they would have to do some kind of penance, like helping Mr Doyle remove the vast quantities of chewing gum stuck to the bottom of classroom tables. Why the children couldn't be made to do this, as punishment for putting the disgusting lumps of sticky, germ ridden goo there in the first place, was a question not worth asking because they knew they would never get a satisfactory answer.

So while the Principal was holding forth about the possibility of a forthcoming inspection, they all looked decidedly glum; Susan Shepherd having the glummest expression of all. She wished she could nod off, like Mr Hill, who was flat out, in his usual position but she couldn't and simply had to listen to her new Principal, who was now in full flow.

"So, I can't impress on staff enough," said Bethany, "the importance of this crucial planning and, I'm going to prove very unpopular I know but, as from next week, I'm insisting on triplicate plans being made for every lesson; a copy for the department, a copy for the inspectors and one for your records. This must include the learning objective and a full breakdown of teaching, stroke, learning activities and success criteria."

Appalled, Dave interrupted, "But we don't know when or even if we're going to be inspected yet, do we? You're creating an enormous amount of extra paperwork for everyone. Why don't we wait until we know when they're coming? Anyway I've been teaching for over twenty years and it's all in here," he said, pointing to his balding head.

"Be that as it may," continued Bethany, "we need to show the inspectors that Southgreen Academy is vigilant and knows exactly where it's going in relation to monitoring its children's educational attainment. Its practice, Dave, practice! So that, when they do turn up we'll be fully prepared. They'll be a pro-forma for everyone on a

CD ROM, so you can do the work at home, which will be available from Sebastian ... when will they be available, Seb?"

"Well, it'll have to be Friday, I suppose," said a particularly disgruntled Sebastian. "Haven't got round to it yet, boss, but no doubt I can while away the next few evenings at home, with nothing better to do than to copy endless CDs. Of course, when I'm going to fit in next year's timetable, God only knows so, if you're all double booked for rooms and teaching two classes at the same time in September, don't blame me, blame ... well, blame bloody OFS- !"

"Thank you, Sebastian, we know how dreadfully overworked you are," said Bethany, "but I would remind you that the particular acronym that you have just tried to use is banned on these premises and I'd also appreciate a little less of the 'bloody.' "

Dave laughed loudly and Bethany asked, "What's funny about that, Mr Hardman?"

"Nothing," replied Dave.

This raised a smile among the support staff who liked Sebastian's free use of swear words, when out of the Principal's earshot, and only wished on occasions like this that they could swear themselves. Susan Shepherd almost giggled but stopped herself just in time. Their expressions all changed however, when Bethany continued speaking.

"And now after the brainstorming and these few crucial words from me comes the bombshell. Though these measures might seem harsh, I can assure you that they are necessary because I have just spoken to Mr Harris, the leader of the team, and he has informed me that our school could well be in line for a snap inspection. From next week, we can expect them at any time."

There were great gasps all round.

Bethany thought that the troops needed rallying, but what she now had to say was said as self-justification rather than to instill rigour and vigour into the hearts of a demoralised staff.

"The less said about the last time they came, the better," she continued. "Of course I wasn't at the helm then. We have swept out the old and whisked in the new and, in the short time I've been here, I've made it quite clear that changes need to be made in every department. Tutor groups have gone and Mentoring Registration Groups have been brought in. Mr Bull and I are exploring every avenue in improving our marketing, vis-a-vis the farm, and how this distinguishes us from other schools. Many more changes are to come. We are an improving school! I feel it and I'm sure you do too. Don't you feel it? Well, don't you?"

There was total silence, evincing an atmosphere of acute indifference, until Bethany was rescued by her trusty cohort and Mr Dylan piped up with, "Yes, boss, we feel it all right. We're on the up. Definitely making slow, I mean, making steady progress."

"Of course we are. Thank you, Mr Dylan. Now has anyone got anything else to say? Mr Hill?"

But, of course Mr Hill had nothing to say, for he was oblivious to the frosty atmosphere in the room, being cosily tucked up in his chair.

Mr Dylan gave him another helping hand however saying, "We had a departmental meeting yesterday and I've made some interesting new proposals for change in the department, which Mr Hill is considering."

"Thank you Mr Dylan," said Bethany, "and, if I may steal a few more minutes of your time, I'll take a look at those in my office immediately after this meeting."

Helga whispered conspiratorially to Dave, "I bet that's not all she wants to take a look at."

But Bethany had the ears of a fox and snapped back, "What was that, Helga?"

"Nothing," replied Helga.

"Anybody else? Support staff? No? Susan?"

Susan shook her head.

"As usual. If I may say, just to round things off, and you know I never like to single people out, but our wonderful support staff always listen so attentively and just get on with it. Don't you? Don't you, Susan?"

There were murmurs of agreement and Susan blushed scarlet, having been, inevitably, singled out.

"You are a credit to our establishment," she continued. "You look after some of our most challenging pupils with all kinds of learning, behavioural and medical difficulties. You never complain, have incredible patience, get moved around from pillar to post and, to top it all, you are never a financial burden on the school because you are paid a paltry pittance which you never, ever complain about. I am truly thankful for that. Where would we be without you? Your quiet and thoughtful approach could be well heeded by other members of staff who are far better qualified and earn a lot more money. Thank you everybody. Mr Dylan, if you would be so kind." With that summons, Mr Dylan followed the Principal into her office and the meeting ended.

"Ten days beyond the sell by date, you say?" said Bethany as she closed the door.

"And there were no other packets in the bin," said Mr Dylan. "I rummaged through. Just some of Mr Hill's empty Cheeselet bags, some penguin wrappers and a few –"

"Alright, alright!" snapped a troubled Bethany, "you don't need to tell me the entire contents of the rubbish bin."

"Sorry, I was only trying to help."

"Yes, I know," replied Bethany, trying to make amends, "and I'm very grateful. Not a word to anyone about this though, Evan."

"No of course not," he replied, encouraged that she'd called him by his first name, something she'd never done before. "Boss," he said tentatively, "I've heard that there are a record number of applicants for Mr Hill's job," gullibly taking Randy Andy's information as gospel.

"I suppose, under the old regime, three candidates would constitute some sort of record but, I have to say, I'm rather disappointed."

"Only three?" asked Evan, relieved to hear that there wasn't much competition.

"Yes, you and two others, both Oxbridge graduates."

"Oxbridge?" asked Evan, now concerned that the competition might be stiff.

"Yes, remind me where you trained, Mr Dylan?"

A little miffed that she had reverted to addressing him with her usual formality, he replied, "Swansea."

"Ah, yes, that's where you're from isn't it?"

"Yes, I was one of the few lucky enough to live at home when I went to university," said the Welshman, mistakenly thinking that this would impress his boss, but she came back with, "So you're a bit of a mummy's boy?"

"Oh, I wouldn't say that, but I'm proud of being a Swansea Jack."

"Sorry?"

"It's what they call people from Swansea, see. Named after a dog that rescued lots of people from a shipwreck."

"So, you're named after a dog?"

"Not exactly, no. It's traditional, see. If you're from Swansea, you have the nickname, whether you're a boy or girl."

"Very quaint. And how long have you been teaching exactly?"

"Eleven years."

"So, you're top of the pay scale."

"Thankfully," replied Swansea Jack.

"That's not so good," frowned Bethany.

"Because?"

"Because, Mr Dylan, the other two candidates are extremely highly qualified Oxbridge scientists, who have only been teaching for two years, so they'd be thousands of pounds a year cheaper to employ than you."

"So you mean I haven't a chance?"

"No, I'd never say that and I would never pre-judge any application procedure; it would be most unethical. Anyway, you have certain other admirable qualities, Evan, such as experience, knowledge of our school systems and, dare I say ... loyalty."

"Thanks boss," said Evan, heartened that the informality had been resumed.

"Confidentially, Evan, I'm very worried about Helga. If she's feeding me rotten éclairs deliberately, then what might she do next? If only I could find out what she's up to next door."

"I agree, boss. It was a sneaky thing to do."

"I can be just as sneaky, Evan. If only I could know what she's planning."

Laughing and not wishing to be taken seriously, Evan said, "Well, you could put a bug in her room; that would do the trick."

"Evan, that's a brilliant idea," said Bethany, delighted he had taken the bait. "How could that be done?"

"Oh, it's easy enough. You'd just need to run a wire through from your room to a tiny mic on her desk that would pick up her voice. You could listen through earphones. You wouldn't want anybody knowing about it though, boss."

"Well, no one would know about it, would they?"

"No, I don't suppose they would."

"I can trust you can't I, Evan?"

"Oh, yes boss, absolutely. Your secret's safe with me."

"I can see that you're an ideas man, Evan. So when can you fix it? Immediately?"

"Fix what?" said Evan.

"The microphone on Helga's desk."

"Me? You want me to do it?"

"Well, you said it would be easy."

Although Mr Dylan knew right from wrong and understood that what was being requested was undoubtedly the latter, he was also buoyed up by the new found trust that the Principal was placing in him, and knew that his sworn secrecy, moreover, would give him a certain leverage with his superior. Besides, he wanted the job of Head of Science and nothing was going to stand in his way, although he knew it was no foregone conclusion that he would succeed, as he was up against two Oxbridge graduates. Indeed, in that moment, he imagined how wonderful it would feel to triumph over them, in his quest for the post. It was therefore, as they say, a 'no-brainer.'

"Okay, boss, I'll do it! I'll do it later, when she's gone home." And with those words the die was cast.

"Thank you, Evan," said Bethany, beaming. "I knew I could count on you. I just knew it."

♦ ♦ ♦

The clock in the staffroom showed 17.00 hours as Dave finished marking another exam paper and put it aside. Françoise Poitin entered and stood near Dave saying, "Mr Hardman, I wonder if I could ask your advice?"

"About what?"

"That boy, Peter Sutcliffe."

"What about him?"

Françoise took out a piece of A4 cartridge paper from her attaché case and passed it to Dave saying, "He did this lovely drawing of me to accompany the poem."

"Yes, it's very good. You as a mermaid; it fits with the verse. There appears to be no end to Peter's talents. So, why do you need my advice?"

"Well, he stopped me this afternoon, in the corridor and asked if he could paint me for his GCSE art project."

"And you said?"

"That I'd think about it."

"That's good."

"It was the way he said it though, that was so charming and rather took me aback, but then he elaborated and said that, he would absolutely understand if I said 'no' but, because the project was supposed to be a life study, artistically, it would be best if I modelled for him in the nude."

"Did he indeed?" said Dave, smiling and almost laughing at the sheer audacity of the poetic artist and namesake of the Yorkshire Ripper.

"I refused, of course," said Françoise, quickly.

"I would have done too," replied Dave, trying to eradicate the image that suddenly sprang into his mind of him standing exposed and naked in front of Peter Sutcliffe's easel. "Very wise," he said. "You could get yourself into a lot of trouble there; you being a teacher and Peter being under sixteen."

"Yes, I know," said Françoise, "but it's a pity in a way, not to be able to help. He was so earnest and so very sincere about it."

"But Peter's earnest and sincere about absolutely everything, Françoise! The difference between you and most of the other teachers, is that they think he's a total pain in the arse."

"Do you agree?"

"Well, they do have a point but, on the other hand, I've always thought Peter a highly intelligent young man with enormous potential."

"Exactly," said Françoise. "And where would Picasso or Goya or Lucien Freud be without the nude? I would have happily modelled for any of them, if they'd have asked."

"I couldn't agree more but this is for Peter's GCSE Art project, not a forthcoming exhibition at the Tate Modern!"

"Yes, but you have to start somewhere."

"But Peter doesn't have to paint *you*. All I'd say is, if you are considering helping him, in any way, don't do anything without talking to Mr Latham, the Head of Art."

"Thanks," said Françoise, as she turned and left the room, almost bumping into Mr Dylan, who was wearing a bright yellow hard hat and carrying a toolbox.

"If it isn't Bob the Builder," said Dave, chuckling at the sight of the silly looking Welshman.

"Oh, yes, very funny," said Mr Dylan, who had hoped everyone would have gone home by now. Holding up his toolbox he added, "And if you're wondering why I'm carrying this around it's because, well I ..." but he became unusually tongue tied and wished he hadn't started to explain.

"Go on," said Dave, "I wasn't wondering but I'm fascinated now."

"Yes, well I, I, well I ..." Mr Dylan stammered, but then looked relieved when he saw Helga leaving her office, carrying her bag.

"Mr Dylan was just explaining, Helga, why he's giving us his uncanny impression of Bob the Builder. Well, Mr Dylan?"

Still not off the hook and embarrassed, Mr Dylan made do with saying, "Just doing some electrical work on circuits and that, see."

"And you have to wear a bright yellow hard hat for that?" enquired Dave.

"Health and Safety, see," said the pedantic Mr Dylan but Dave looked doubtful and said, "You scientists really know how to have a good time."

"He was having a very good time earlier," said Helga. "You should have seen him, Dave. He says he was performing the Heimlich Manoeuvre on Ms Sedgeford but that's not what it looked like to me."

"I was, Helga, honest –"

But Helga cut him off and said, "If I'd come in a few moments earlier I daresay he'd have been giving her mouth to mouth resuscitation!"

"She was choking," pleaded the now red-faced Mr Dylan, "I thought she'd got something stuck in her throat."

"And what might that have been?" asked Helga. "A bit of Welsh rarebit?" But Swansea Jack didn't know where to put himself as Helga said, "Perish the thought. Anyway, I'm off home now, in search of some normality. I shall see you both back at the madhouse, bright and early in the morning." And with that, Helga left Mr Dylan and Mr Hardman to themselves.

"She ought to watch herself, that one," said Mr Dylan after she'd gone.

"Oh, yes?"

"New broom sweeps clean and all that."

"Especially when the wicked witch is sitting astride the broomstick," replied Dave, before gathering his exam papers and making a quick exit. "I'm off too. Going to catch the end of my son's cricket match," he said, not giving Mr Dylan the chance to say goodbye. Fifteen minutes later, Dave would regret his haste, as he had left his keys on the table where he'd been marking. En route to his car, he was waylaid by a distraught Mr Doyle, and it was only after offering some insincere sympathy to the caretaker about his spelling mistake and his consequential enrolment onto an adult literacy course, at the Principal's instigation, that he was able to return to the staff room to rescue his keys.

During this time, Mr Dylan, seeing that the coast was now clear, had started to install the tiny mic, concealed beneath the rear of a framed photo of Helga's children, which sat upon her desk. He ran the thin black wire down the inside of the black metal desk leg so that Helga would never see it. The next bit was trickier as he had to raise the carpet so than he could run the wire underneath. Luckily, he had some double sided tape so, once he'd positioned the wire correctly, he was able to replace the carpet without Helga, or anyone else for that matter, being able to see that it had been tampered with. Once through the door into Bethany's office, it was an easy matter to run the wire along the base of the skirting and then up the leg of the Principal's desk. He drilled a tiny hole into the side of the top drawer of the desk and inserted the wire. He was rather proud of this concealment. All that remained was for him to solder the female part of the jack to the end of the wire and then it would be easy for earphones to be inserted, so that Ms Sedgeford could listen in on whatever future subterfuge Helga might be planning. He knew the morality of this course of action was questionable, to say the least, but justified it by accepting that the new Principal had arrived at a desperately difficult time for Southgreen and that desperate times required desperate measures. Besides, he had more or less been ordered to carry out the task and it would do his chances of promotion no harm at all. The end, he surmised, would justify the means.

While the bugging device was being installed, Randy Andy had come into the staff room. He lifted his mug, emblazoned with his name in large red letters, from one of the hooks and spooned some coffee into it. Then he filled it with boiling water from the dispenser and grabbed a carton of milk from the fridge. He sniffed it before adding some to his coffee. Replacing the milk in the fridge he took a sip and then wandered over to a table, putting the mug down. He stood looking down at the magazines on the table and was unaware of the silent Julia, who crept up behind him and covered his eyes with her hands. Thinking it was Françoise, he smiled and said, "Je t'aime, mon amour."

"Oh, I find French talk very sexy," whispered Julia.

Now, realising his mistake, his expression turned to one of shock and he said, "Julia, I wasn't expecting you."

"No, I thought you'd be surprised." She wrapped her arms around him and started to kiss him, slipping her tongue into his mouth but he drew back saying, "No, not here."

"Don't be silly," she said, "most of them have gone home." She tried to kiss him again but he resisted saying, "You never know who might still be hanging about."

"Let's go to your room then."

"Not just now, Julia-"

"But it's been hours, Andy. Please? You know I won't disappoint the Grand Old Duke of York. I'll do anything his lordship asks."

Put like that, how could Randy Andy resist. They kissed again and this time his hands roamed over her breasts and then, down her back and all over her bum, coming to a sudden halt when he heard, Linda Baker's unmistakable voice screeching, "You bastard!"

She was standing in the doorway looking ashen, as the other two broke from their embrace. Andy could only say, pathetically, "I thought you were sick."

"Sick? Me? Oh, yes, I'm sick alright," replied Linda. "Sick of the sight of you sliding your grubby hands all over her tight little arse!"

"Thanks for the compliment," said Julia.

Putting the final touches to his handiwork, Mr Dylan had heard the noise coming from the staff room and now had his ear pressed firmly to the door, as Andy said, "Linda, this is not the time or the place-" but was cut off immediately by Linda who shouted, "Don't you start telling me what I can and can't do. I came here because I needed to talk to you in private."

"Anything you want to say you can say in front of Julia," said Andy, trying to take control.

"Oh, I don't think so," said Linda. "You're making a big mistake. I don't think Little Miss Muffet here is going to want to hear what I have to say."

"I'll go, Andy," said Julia but he stopped her saying,

"No, stay. I've told you, Linda, it's over between us. There was never anything there in the first place. It was just a bit of fun but you couldn't understand that, could you? I told you time and time again but you just had to start getting possessive and making demands and –" but before he could finish Linda broke down sobbing, saying,

"I loved you. I really loved you, Andy. I told you ... and now –" but she broke down again and all Andy could say was, "Linda, don't, please ... not here."

Through her tears she said, "You don't understand, Andy. You can't possibly understand."

"What, Linda? What don't I understand?"

"It's not possible," she sobbed. "You'll never understand!"

"What, Linda? What?" he asked again, bewildered.

"I'm pregnant! I'm carrying your child. *Your* baby, Andy. Our baby."

With all the sensitivity that rotten Randy Andy could muster he said, "Well, I'm really sorry about that but you told me it was safe and that you didn't think you could get pregnant, so you can hardly blame me for –"

"Oh, of course, it's not your fault," snapped Linda. "It couldn't possibly be your fault, could it?"

"Well, have you seen a doctor? It's quite a straightforward procedure these days," said Andy, now patronising his ex-lover. "If you want to go private and get it done quicker, then of course -"

But before he could do any more damage Linda slapped him, with the full force of her outstretched, swinging palm, hitting him on his left cheek.

"There was no need for that," said Julia but Linda hadn't finished.

"Oh, yes, there was," she said. "Private? Get it done quicker? He knows perfectly well that Charlie and I were trying for eight years to have a baby. We went through three courses of IVF for Christ's sake, but it didn't work and we split up with the strain of it. And now the bastard expects me to have an abortion! Well, I'm not going to. Do you hear me, Andy? I won't!"

As Dave entered, hearing the shouting before he arrived, he was confronted by the sight of Julia, slapping Andy, just as hard as Linda had done a moment earlier, around his right cheek. Andy's future was looking decidedly less rosy than his face was at that second, as Julia burst into tears and ran out of the room.

"Dave, thank God you're here. I'm pregnant. I'm carrying Andy's child," said Linda Baker, the depressed Head of Maths.

Dave stood, flabbergasted by what he had walked into, inwardly digesting and savouring the unusual sensation of seeing the Head of PE getting his comeuppance. It was a moment he would remember. He looked at Andy and said, "Forgot my keys," then, unable to look Linda in the eye, he left.

Mr Dylan, Swansea Jack, otherwise known to staff and students alike as Mr Tambourine Man, had been riveted by the information that he'd just heard, while listening from behind the door of the Principal's office. He resolved to get in extra early in the morning to report back to his boss exactly what had happened, while carrying out her oh so, very, necessary bugging installation. He waited till everyone had disappeared and then slipped out, like Bob the Builder.

On his way to the car park, Dave had managed to avoid another counselling session, mentoring Mr Doyle. Getting into his car he stretched out his hand to turn on the CD. Rather appropriately, the iconoclastic guitar sounds of The Incredible String Band blossomed, not tamely but hugely, from the speakers, as he drove out of the school gates. Listening to the lyrics that alluded to an artist delving into his box of paints and only choosing the shades and colours of his loved one, Dave chuckled, thinking what an amazing boy Peter Sutcliffe was. Asking the French teacher to pose naked for him! Writing her a poem and drawing her as a mermaid. That's what he called potential. What more was there to come? This was the question that Dave Hardman pondered over, as he drove to watch his son play cricket, on the first day of term six.

Randy Andy's day however was far from over. The news of his possible fatherhood had stunned him and he didn't know what to do. He made his way to his office and, as he entered, saw the forlorn figure of Julia, sitting in his swivel chair. She held a key up in front of her face.

"You ought to have this back," she said, stoically.

"Julia, you have to understand. It's not my fault. She told me she couldn't have children. I was straight with her."

"Yes, but –"

"Please don't do this," he continued. "I know I might have been a little hard on her but I'd told her it was over so many times. I've been straight with you, Julia, too. Honestly. Please, I don't want us to finish. Please, keep the key."

She held out the key to him, as if she were insisting he should take it. He stretched out his hand hesitantly, but then she snatched the key away and put it in the pocket of her tracksuit, smiling. He smiled back as she said, "You're going to have to make it up to me."

"Oh, don't worry, I will," replied Andy. "Look, don't you think it would be better at the moment if we saw each other away from school?"

"Maybe you're right," said Julia, spinning through three hundred and sixty degrees and then rising from the chair. "One last time though?"

How could he refuse? They kissed passionately. Frantic now, they couldn't wait and made their way towards the shower room, undressing as they went, pulling at their clothes and kissing each newly exposed piece of flesh.

"Oh, yes, Andy, I want you," said Julia.

"And the Grand Old Duke of York wants his Little Miss Muffet," said Andy.

They giggled as Andy turned on the shower and they entered, kissing and touching each other intimately, as the water and steam enveloped them both and they began what was their second session of wet, soapy sex together that day. If Julia was unsure about the state of Andy's relationship with Linda, she was completely unaware that, for Andy, this was his third sexual encounter of the day, as he'd also had sex, not for the first time, with Françoise Poitin. But their bodies were now entwined and they were so wrapped up in themselves that neither of them were aware of the sound of a gentle knock on Andy's office door.

"Andy? Andy, are you in there?" said Françoise, in a forced whisper. She knocked again but there was no response. She cupped her ear against the door but could only hear the sound of running water. Unlike Julia, Andy had not furnished her with a key. She looked at her watch and waited for a moment before turning round and walking back along the corridor.

As she got into her 2CV with the stripy red, white and blue roof, she sat for a moment, thinking. She took the poem that Peter Sutcliffe had written for her out of her attaché case, along with the picture he'd drawn of her as a mermaid. She read the poem again and smiled. She looked at the picture with admiration. She would get it framed. What a curious and talented boy he was, she thought. Her mind turned to Andy. Could she trust him? She wasn't sure but suspicion had been sown. Was he telling her the truth about having finished with Julia? She was determined to find out. As she started the car and released the handbrake, she pressed the play button on the old cassette player. The sound of Annie Lennox's wonderful, strident voice, singing about lying men being sharp thorns that could prick and hurt gave her pause for thought. Could the song be prophetic? She wondered if it was, as she stepped on the accelerator and sped out of the gates of Southgreen Academy, at the end of another day.

PART TWO

THE ROCKET MAN ET LE JOUR DE GLOIRE

The digital clock in the staff room read 08:10 hours on Monday, June 8th. As Dave was cursing, putting toner in the photocopier, Françoise appeared at his shoulder and said, "Dave, Peter Sutcliffe's waiting in the corridor. He wants you."

"Tell him I'm busy would you please, Françoise."

"Of course," said Françoise, who left to pass the message on to Peter.

Dave managed to replace the toner cartridge, but then realised that there was a paper jam and came up with several choice expletives that Basil would have been proud of, before pulling the offending paper out, suffering a paper cut on his index finger and pressing the start button. Nothing happened. Dave swore again, sucked his bleeding finger and kicked the machine. He took a deep breath, pressed the start button once more and the copier finally did Dave's bidding and actually copied the documents he needed for his first lesson.

Françoise returned, holding a bunch of leaflets. "Peter said, could you put these into teachers' pigeon holes?"

"Did he indeed?" replied Dave. "Sounds ominous."

Giving Dave the leaflets she added, "He says that you are the only member of staff who understands."

Dave began reading the leaflet and started to laugh.

"What's so funny?" asked Françoise.

Dave then proceeded to give a running commentary on the piece of powerful propaganda that he was now holding in his hands. "Here listen to this," he said.

"'Stop animal experimentation now!!!' Triple exclamation mark. 'Stop animal exploitation now!!!' Triple exclamation mark. 'Did you know that if all the grazing land in the world was turned over to crop production there would be enough food to feed every human being on the planet? STOP GRAZING AND RAISING ANIMALS AT SOUTHGREEN ACADEMY NOW!!!' Triple exclamation mark and capital letters. *'WE MUST NOT KILL AND HARM ANIMALS FOR FOOD OR FOR MEDICAL RESEARCH!!!!'* Quadruple exclamation mark, capital letters and italics. 'WE ARE THE SOUTHGREEN ANIMAL LIBERATION ARMY for MORAL INTEGRITY!!!!!' Five exclamation marks and capital letters. 'WATCH THIS SPACE.' He's slipped up there."

"Why?" asked Françoise.

"His rather inappropriate acronym spells out the word SALAMI," replied Dave, laughing out loud.

Françoise laughed too and said, "Oh, I don't know, Dave, maybe he meant it?"

"Come to think of it, you're probably right. Not only a political activist but a polished satirist as well."

"You're forgetting poet and artist too. Are you going to do what he asked?"

"Of course. Anything for a laugh to start the week. Keep a look out will you."

Françoise stood by the main door of the staff room and watched to see that no one was coming, while Dave started to put a leaflet into every staff pigeon hole.

Meanwhile, Helga entered the Principal's office through the door from the corridor, knowing that Bethany was talking to Mr Dylan in the science lab. She crossed through the adjoining door to her office and placed her bag by her chair. She looked at the framed photo of her adorable little children, which sat on her desk and wondered how those two delightful babies had turned into the morose and lazy teenagers that they now were. She was about to pick up the photo frame but thought better of it and consoled herself with the knowledge that she had gleaned from an article in one of Bethany's old copies of "Hello" magazine, which said that teenagers were hormonally pre-destined to need more sleep and that their parents should just learn to live with it. That was all very well, she thought, but it didn't make Monday mornings any easier.

Françoise signalled to Dave that people were approaching, so he stuffed the last few SALAMI leaflets into the pigeon holes and quickly sat down.

"That's a splendid idea, Evan," said Bethany, entering the staff room, with her Welsh cohort and Sebastian. "You can explain it to the others at the briefing." This new found informality was not wasted on Sebastian, who was not sure he even knew that Mr Tambourine Man actually had a first name. Bethany crossed to her office, admiring the new sign, now spelt correctly, that adorned the door. As she entered, she made a mental note to compliment Mr Doyle on his work, to show him that there were no hard feelings, at the same time reminding herself to check when the first session of the adult literacy course, he was now enrolled on, was scheduled for.

As soon as the Welshman was out of earshot, Sebastian muttered, "Creep," to himself and then said, sotto voce, "Where was I? Ah, yes. Check, check and check again." He then emptied his pigeon hole and started to look through the contents.

"Would you fucking credit it, Dave, Carl Borman's got a referral from the Lolly Pop Lady, passed on by reception and it's only fucking twenty past eight. It's his first day back after exclusion for Christ's sake."

"What did he do?" asked Dave.

"Walked straight in front of a car on the Panda crossing and then shouted abuse at the poor motorist doing an emergency stop, before giving the 'zeig heil' sign to the irate Lolly Pop Lady and shouting, 'Achtung. Raus. Raus!' What boxes shall I tick?"

"Do we have one for morbid fixation on inappropriate role models?" said Dave.

"Well, that's a two hour after school detention for our little, fascist thug and he's not even penetrated the barbed wire yet!" said Sebastian. "Now," he continued, "what's this? Good God! Have you seen this leaflet, Dave?"

"Leaflet?" said Dave, playing dumb.

"The one that appears to be in all the pigeon holes?" said Sebastian.

"No."

"Have you, Mademoiselle Poitin?"

"No, I haven't checked my pigeon hole yet, Basil," said Françoise.

Sebastian, smarting at the mention of his nickname nevertheless felt triumphant at the thought of having evidence to use against Peter. "Yes, it has to be," he said. "Got him at last. Let's see how our serial rapist killer, Mr Sutcliffe, tries to wheedle his way out of this one." And with those words he entered the Principal's office.

Françoise turned and whispered, "I do hope you're not going to get Peter into trouble, Dave."

Dave smiled, tapped his nose and said, "Listen and watch."

♦ ♦ ♦

All the usual people were there at the briefing, except for one. Mr Hill's chair was empty. The support staff were gossiping about him, since he wasn't there to hear them and Susan Shepherd got quite animated at one point, recounting a particular story about Mr Hill, a Bunsen burner and a poor boy in Year 9 who had had his fringe singed and whose mother had tried to sue the school and Mr Hill for negligence. Susan said that the mother had settled for a Christmas Turkey hamper, and no more was ever said about it, which only illustrated that the new Principal, being a woman with three degrees and a serving Justice of the Peace, was not the first person to use the school farm as a grubby means to an end, which was ultimately beneficial to the school, whichever way you looked at it. So when the new Principal held forth, as she was doing now, about the considerable changes she was making, Susan Shepherd thought, though she'd never admit it, that she'd seen it all before and that nothing ever really changed.

"So, I would remind staff, on pain of a slow death that, from period one today, you must have a lesson plan available, in triplicate, for each class you teach. You can also expect me to interrupt you at any time, as the inspectors will do, to see this directive is being observed. I trust you all got your CD ROMS from Sebastian on Friday?"

Sebastian chipped in with, "Yes, boss. It only took me till after Question Time on Thursday night to finish them but 'je ne regret rien.'"

"No problems, I take it," said Bethany, checking.

Andy Bailey had lots on his mind, so this was just another irritant. "Yes, actually, there is a problem," he said. "I couldn't do any lesson planning over the weekend because all that the CD ROM, Sebastian gave me, had installed on it was the framework for next year's draft timetable!"

"Good God, that's where it got to," said Sebastian. "I was searching for that all day Sunday. Seeing that you've got it perhaps you'd like to finish the job for me. It'll only take you the next six weeks but it'll make a change from synchronised gymnastics or whatever else it is you get up to down there in PE."

"Thank you, Sebastian," said Bethany. "And now I'll hand you over to Mr Dylan, who has a splendid idea that he wants to put to you all. Evan." And indeed it was a splendid idea that would have ramifications and creative possibilities that no one could predict at this stage but it was, without a doubt, something that Mr Tambourine Man was going to sell to staff and pupils alike.

"Thanks, boss," said Mr Dylan. He continued in a friendly yet slightly sombre way. "Well, colleagues, you'll have noticed that Mr Hill is not sat in his customary chair. Unfortunately, he's got a hospital appointment today but it's rather opportune because what I have to say is not for his ears. Staff who have been here some time will remember that Mr Hill used to run a rocket competition every year. This involved a lunchtime and after school club, in which chemistry students used to make all kinds of pyrotechnics, culminating in a wonderful firework display. Mr Hill judged the winners and there were prizes for all. So, what I propose is that I will supervise students who want to take part in a similar event, and Ms Sedgeford has agreed that we can hold a surprise firework display, in Mr Hill's honour, on the evening of the Summer Fair, in the last week of term."

"How are we going to keep it secret?" asked Dave.

"Good point, Mr Hardman. Could Group Tutors –"

"Uh, uh, uh, Mr Dylan, you're forgetting," said Bethany.

"Sorry, boss, I meant to say could Group Mentors inform students about this at Mentoring Registration today and stress how important secrecy is. The code word for the project will be 'sparkler' and students who are interested should come to the science lab at 12.45 today. If Mr Hill does get wind of it, I'll tell him we're making sparklers for Guy Fawkes Night, and he'll be miffed because that's in term two next year, when he won't be here. That'll make it even more of a surprise when the big event cracks off in July."

"Thank you, Evan," said Bethany, adding, "I'm sure we'll be able to give Mr Hill the send-off he deserves. Any questions?"

"Yes," said Dave. "Will Mr Hill be going up in one of these rockets?"

This drew widespread laughter from everybody and Susan Shepherd nearly fell off her chair.

"Oh, you are awful, Dave, really," said Bethany. "Seb, I believe you've got a couple of things to say."

"Yes, boss," said Sebastian. "First, I'm afraid to say that our drama teacher, Mr Wiseman, is in plaster for the next six weeks with a broken left fibula, so that's him off till September, lucky bugger."

"Sebastian!" warned Bethany.

"Sorry, boss. I meant lucky so and so. Fortunately, Mr Carter, our very own, home grown thespian, has agreed to hold the fort, unless of course Steven Spielberg rings with a better offer. Mr Carter will be unavailable however this Friday as he has an audition for ... what is it for, Mr Carter, remind me?"

"A pot noodles ad," answered Tom.

"That's the one," said Sebastian, "playing the part, if my memory is correct, of a pornographic film maker, auditioning a scantily clad woman and asking her to drip noodles all down her cleavage."

There was widespread laughter again. The staff loved it when Sebastian talked like this and he was on top form this morning and went on, saying, "If I may venture to offer a word of advice, Mr Carter, for one so young, you seem to be getting easily type cast."

Tom took being Sebastian's stooge all in good humour, for the first rule of being an actor, as he had learnt from bitter experience, was that you had to be able to take a joke. Playing a nine foot penis at the Edinburgh Festival had gone a long way in teaching him that!

"Secondly," continued Sebastian, "if anyone has any idea who put these seditious, terrorist leaflets in pigeon holes or who are the individuals involved in the 'Southgreen Animal Liberation Army for Moral Integrity,' could they please see me as soon as -" but he was cut off by Dave who simply said, "SALAMI."

"Sorry, Dave?"

"It spells SALAMI."

"What does?" asked Sebastian, looking at the leaflet again and sounding out the words. "Southgreen Animal Liberation Army for Moral – oh, I see! SALAMI!"

"It has to be a joke," confirmed Dave.

Gradually, all the staff started to laugh, as they worked out the acronym for themselves. The laughter built and even Bethany joined in, finally followed by Basil, who then went way over the top and laughed so loudly and forcefully that snot almost came out of his nose.

Bethany concluded what had turned out to be a rather raucous briefing saying, "Teachers, please look at the exam invigilation timetable carefully. Anything else from anybody? Support staff? Susan? No, as usual. Have a nice day everyone!"

♦ ♦ ♦

The staff room had emptied and Françoise found herself alone. Andy must have been somewhere close by, because his sports bag had been left on one of the chairs. Françoise looked to see if anyone was coming and then rifled through the bag, quickly removing a set of keys. She put them in her attaché case just as he returned.

"Did I leave my bag? Ah, there it is" he said. "Forget my head –"

"If it wasn't screwed on. Isn't that good colloquial speech?" asked Françoise.

"Très bien Mademoiselle. C'est parfait," replied Randy Andy.

"Your French is improving."

"Yes, I know all the days of the week and I can count up to sixty nine."

"You've got a one track mind."

"But I'm nowhere near the finish line with you." Andy went to kiss Françoise but she drew away.

"Not here," she said. "Do you have your head screwed on, Andy?"

"What? Look, babe, no one's about."

Although Françoise now knew about Linda being pregnant by Andy and he had told her it was over with her and that Julia was also only a fling from the recent past, she needed reassurance.

"You promise me you're not still seeing Julia?"

"I promise. I told you babe, she came to collect some stuff she left after school last week. Then Linda saw her and that's why it all kicked off with her. I promise I'm being straight with you, ma cherie."

"You'd better be, Andy because I won't be responsible for my actions if you're not."

"Anyway, I've got to go. I'm looking forward to this. I'm going to teach that Peter Sutcliffe a lesson he'll never forget."

"What are you going to do?"

"Asking you to pose nude for him indeed. He's going to wish he'd never laid there all those nights thinking about it."

"I wish I'd never told you. Don't do anything to Peter, Andy, do you hear? He's a very clever young man!"

But Andy didn't care about Peter and couldn't wait to make life difficult for him, so he left Françoise saying, "Au revoir, ma cherie."

As soon as he'd gone Françoise took a business card from her pocket along with her mobile phone. She made a call. "Hello, I brought in some shoes to be heeled yesterday and wondered if they're ready? ... Poitin ... they are? Thanks, I'll come and pick them up right now. One more thing." Françoise looked around and lowered her voice, "I believe you cut keys too ... yes, do you do it while you wait? ... Thanks, I'll be ten minutes."

◆ ◆ ◆

For the last few days Bethany had been listening in on Helga next door, through an earpiece plugged in to the wire and connector in the top drawer of her desk. Nothing remarkable had occurred and she had begun to think that the chocolate éclair episode had been an aberration and that Mr Dylan's splendid bugging handiwork had not been necessary. She was however going to be disabused of this shortly as, when she inserted the earpiece, she could hear that Helga was on the phone and, within seconds, she realised that she was talking to Mr Harris, the Chief Inspector.

"Hello Mr Harris, it's Ms Sedgeford's secretary, Helga, just returning your call."

Bethany didn't know he'd called before because Helga hadn't told her. She was cross.

"No, I'm afraid she's busy just now and doesn't want to be disturbed. Can I help at all?" asked Helga.

Bethany was now not only cross but looking very serious, as she hadn't told Helga any such thing. She was also worried about what was coming next and had good cause to be.

"Well between you and me, Mr Harris and strictly confidentially, of course, if you want my opinion ... no, well I know I shouldn't say really ... oh, thank you Mr Harris ... yes ... yes, that's exactly what old Mr Foulkes used to say, 'if you want to know what's really going on in a school ask the secretary or the caretaker.' Yes ... great minds, eh? As I was going to say, Mr Harris, I'd get your team down here as soon as possible if I were you."

Bethany was now so angry that the veins were standing out in her neck. She wanted to go next door and scream at her disloyal secretary but she knew she couldn't and so pressed the earpiece into her ear, holding it firmly in place with her fingers. She knew there was more to come and she didn't want to miss any of it, difficult as it was for her to stomach.

"I'm not saying change is wrong, Mr Harris, believe you me," said Helga, "but it's the wrong things that are getting changed. It never got as bad as this in Mr Foulkes' day. Some of the behaviour is out of control and not just the students either. The Head of Maths has been off with depression and now it appears that she's carrying the Head of PE's baby, and that's not the half of it. He wants nothing to do with her and she won't have an abortion after years of IVF with her previous, so the depression will probably segue nicely into maternity leave and more than likely post-natal depression will set in, so that takes care of the Maths department for the next year ... yes, Mr Harris, yes ... well it's a core subject isn't it?"

Bethany was now fuming and moved to the door, forgetting that the earpiece was in, as it shot out of her ear and fell back into the desk drawer. She could hear Helga saying, "Yes, I know ... I know ... I know," as she opened the connecting door aggressively and said firmly, "Helga, I need you to do something for me NOW!"

Helga smiled at Bethany, which infuriated her even more, and said, "She's actually here now if you'd like to have a word." She held her hand over the mouthpiece and said, "It's that nice Mr Harris on the line."

"I know," said Bethany, quickly realising her mistake and followed it with, "I'll take it in there."

"I'm just passing her over to you," continued Helga. "Yes, it has indeed ... yes I will, I'm sure. I'll see you soon, anyway," now it was

Helga's turn to give away too much information, so she qualified it by adding, "I mean probably sometime in the future, yes."

Bethany returned to her desk to talk to Mr Harris, safe in the knowledge that Helga couldn't be party to the conversation.

"Hello, Mr Harris ... yes ... yes, I know. I have to say that I'd rather you talked directly to me than listen to tittle-tattle from Helga ... well it sounded serious to me from what she was saying ... I could hear, the door was ajar ... yes, yes, I understand ... but I am the Principal of Southgreen Academy and I am trying to turn things round under very difficult circumstances ... yes ... of course, I know you understand ... today? What time? ...Yes, that would be fine, Mr Harris ... yes, clear the air ... preliminary visits are always helpful ... yes, get the layout too ... Yes, I'll still be here ... see you then."

Bethany seemed to have done the trick. Being assertive with the Inspector was the right approach. There was a knock at her door from Helga but Bethany shouted, "I do not want to be disturbed!"

◆ ◆ ◆

At break time Dave was chatting to Tom.

"Good morning so far?" he asked.

"Very," said Tom. "Year 7 then Year 9. They loved it. Makes such a difference when you're taking your own subject."

"Well make a teacher out of you yet."

"No chance."

Andy and Françoise were standing near the door.

"Well, at least that pillock, Sutcliffe won't be giving anyone earache for the rest of the day."

Sebastian caught the end of this as he entered the staff room, saying, "That's where you're incorrect, Mr Bailey, because the very same Peter Sutcliffe has already given me earache and is waiting in the corridor as we speak. I could hardly understand a word he was saying, he was wheezing so much; says can he have his asthma inhaler?"

"Tell him to sod off would you, Seb. I'll get it in a bit. I've left it in my office so he'll just have to wait."

"My pleasure or should I say, plaisir, Mademoiselle," replied Sebastian, looking at Françoise. Turning to Andy he said, "And as for the CD ROM of the draft timetable, I daresay you've left that in your office too?"

"Yeah."

"Fine," said Sebastian. Well I suppose I'll just have to drag myself down to PE sometime later and pick it up. Oh, and I nearly forgot; a present from Reception. I believe these keys belong to you."

Taking the keys, Andy said, "Thanks mate, I've been looking for those all morning; had to get the spare from Mr Doyle."

Sebastian made to leave but Andy stopped him.

"Oh and Basil."

"How many fucking times have I asked you not to fucking well call me that?"

"Sorry, Seb, it's habit. Bit like you saying 'fuck' every other word. Just to say, don't forget to bring the correct CD this time."

"Yes, alright, alright! Isn't anyone allowed a slip up now and then? Oh, everybody, yes but not the fucking Vice Principal." And with those words Sebastian left, only to be heard screaming, "Sutcliffe!" as soon as he entered the corridor.

"What did you do to Peter, Andy?" asked Françoise.

"I made him do one lap of the field and then gave him the chance to apologise for asking you to pose nude for him but he wouldn't; he just said, 'it's none of your business.' So I made him do another lap and then another and ... another –"

"Andy, how could you?"

"It was quite easy, really," said Andy, taking Peter's inhaler out of his track suit bottoms and juggling it. He went on, "Amazingly, he did twelve laps without ever apologising. Must have some crush on you. He'll make the cross country team at this rate!"

But Françoise snatched the inhaler, in mid-air, as Andy threw it up and she strutted out of the staff room.

Andy called after her, "Françoise, it was only a bit of fun. Françoise!" But she'd gone.

Meanwhile Bethany crossed through to Helga's office. Helga needed some papers signing and said, "Ms Sedgeford, I wonder if you could –" but Bethany rode over her saying, "Not now, Helga!" She was greeted in the staff room by Mr Dylan.

"Ah, Evan, just the man," said Bethany. "You'll be pleased to know that the interviews for Mr Hill's job will be held on Tuesday 30th June."

"That's a weight off my mind. It's the not knowing that gets to you."

"Oh, don't go losing sleep over it, Evan. You've got stiff competition but I'm sure you'll do your best."

"Thanks, boss," said the rather relieved Welshman.

As Bethany marched past Helga, she said, "Ms Sedgeford, if you could?–" and was rebuffed yet again with a curt, "I said, not now Helga!" Of course Helga had no idea why Bethany was in such a foul mood and put it down to the possibility of things not having gone well during the conversation with the Chief Inspector.

Françoise was also in a foul mood when she returned to the staff room and confronted Andy.

"The poor boy was totally out of breath. How could you be so cruel?"

"Oh, come on, Françoise, I was only having a laugh."

"Well, I don't think it's very funny."

"I'm sorry. How can I make it up to you?"

"I'm not sure that I want you to."

"Oh, don't be like that. Tell you what, I'm playing Dick at squash after school. Should be finished by five thirty - quarter to six. Why don't you hang around and I'll take you to that new wine bar in town?"

"Only if you promise to leave Peter alone in future?"

He turned to go and said, "Promise. Meet you here at quarter to six." But what Françoise didn't see was that Andy had his fingers crossed behind his back.

♦ ♦ ♦

Tom and Dave were having lunch at The Royal Oak; two perfect pints lined up on the bar in front of them.

"Why are you looking so cheerful?" asked Dave.

"Isn't it allowed, after double drama with the GCSE class that includes Peter Sutcliffe and Carl Borman?"

"Not a viable combination at all. Combustible, I'd say," said Dave.

"That's what I thought too but no, quite the opposite,"

"But Carl Borman hates Peter Sutcliffe; it's well known. He frequently beats him up. I can hardly wait to hear what happened."

"Well," said Tom, "I told them a bit about myself and said that I was an actor and they asked me what I'd been in and I said, 'The Bill' and they asked me what part I'd played and I was very direct and said, 'a dreadful paedophile who had raped a young girl.'"

"You didn't tell them you'd played a nine foot penis at the Edinburgh Festival, then?"

"No," said Tom, "I thought it was a bit too soon for that. Anyway, at first they went totally quiet and then they started to laugh and then the jokes began and Carl Borman shouted, 'Nonce' and 'shirt lifter' and I took it all in good humour but then it went eerily quiet again, so I set them their task."

"Which was?"

"I said they could pick any size group and that they had to create an improvised play about something that really mattered in their life."

"Bet you took hours at home dreaming that one up. Did you do your inspection plan?"

"In triplicate. Anyway, there was the usual ten minutes where they all swapped ideas and formed groups and changed around and, over in one group, Carl Borman was going on and on about doing something about the Nazis, but was getting absolutely nowhere with the others until, at last, Peter Sutcliffe, taking a few gasps on his puffer, said that he'd read this amazing book about the fall of Berlin and that he knew all about it and wanted to direct the play, and that it was a brilliant idea that Carl had had. So, that was it, Peter managed to enthuse the whole group, and they set the play in Hitler's bunker, as the Russian guns closed in."

"Amazing," said Dave.

"You've not heard the half of it. There was nearly a violent row because Carl demanded that he did the scene where Hitler shoots his dog, and Peter was upset, understandably, about this act of wanton cruelty to animals, and said that he didn't think Hitler actually shot the dog himself, indeed Peter seemed to think that the dog had been poisoned."

"Which it had," said Dave.

"But Carl insisted that Hitler had shot it and said he'd beat Peter up if he didn't let him do it. So, Peter said that it was okay because, anyway, it was dramatic license, and though none of the others understood what that meant, they decided to do it anyway."

"Blimey. And?"

"Well Carl got totally immersed in the character of Hitler and Peter was saying things like, 'Just think what it would be like to shoot your own dog, Carl.' And then he asked, 'Carl, do you have a dog?' And Carl said that he did have a dog, called Terry, and Peter got Carl to do the scene again, imagining the dog was Terry. And Carl was nearly crying with the emotion of it all, but when he came to the crucial moment he said, in a funny but convincing German accent, 'Terry, I'm going to have to shoot you now –' and Peter stopped Carl in mid flow and said that it was very good acting, but he only wanted Carl to *imagine* Terry, and that Hitler wouldn't really have had a dog called Terry. Anyway, neither of them knew the name of the real dog, but they knew that Hermann was a common German name because of Hermann Goering and Hermann Goebbels."

"I thought it was Joseph Goebbels?" said Dave.

"It was; they got it wrong. Anyway, they decided to call the dog Hermann but, the next time they did it, Peter said it would be good if they had a person to play Hermann, and Ricky Knapp said that he would do it because he didn't want a speaking role. So Peter said that was okay, but he might have to whimper a bit, and Ricky agreed and they did it!"

"And?" said Dave.

"Well, Ricky's whimpering was so very realistic and performed with such surprisingly effective pathos, that Carl got more and more convincing in his role as Hitler, and when he came to the line, he said, in an improving and now very believable German accent, 'Hermann, I'm going to have to shoot you now,' and Ricky did this excruciatingly sad, final whimper and Carl slowly pulled the trigger, shouting 'Auf Wiedersehen, Hermann!' Then Ricky sprang back and lay stock still, while Carl started to weep over his dead dog's body."

"Incredible," said Dave.

"Yes, it was Dave, but it carried on! Suddenly we realised that Carl *was actually crying* and, then he really broke down and said that Hitler was a bastard for shooting the dog, and that he hated Hitler for doing it, and that he wasn't really crying, only acting. And everyone, including me, praised Carl for his great performance and Ricky too. Then Peter said, 'Yes, I despise the Nazi fascists. They kill dogs and caused the Holocaust and Goebbels poisoned his entire family,' which set Carl off again and he said that Peter was a real mate, that he loved Drama now and that they'd improvise the death of Goebbels' family tomorrow. So they all agreed and that was that!"

♦ ♦ ♦

Later in the afternoon, Helga was putting on her coat. Bethany came through the adjoining door and said, "Slipping off early again, Helga?"

"My watch says five o'clock."

"I think you'll find it's five to," insisted Bethany. "I'm expecting Mr Harris on a quick preliminary visit, to clear the air and to get to grips with the geography of the school."

"You didn't tell me about that," said Helga. Shall I wait and make him a drink or something?"

"No, that won't be necessary. Just show him straight through when he gets here."

At that moment there was a knock on the door.

"That's probably him now," said Bethany. "Come in."

Mr Harris entered and was accompanied by an imposing looking woman, with dark hair, wearing large, horn rimmed glasses.

"Ah, Ms Sedgeford," he said, "I hope you don't mind, but I've brought along my colleague, Dr Sonia Sims. She's one of our most experienced inspectors."

"Pleased to meet you, Ms Sedgeford. I've heard a lot about you," said Dr Sims.

"Pleased to meet you too, Dr Sims," said Bethany, though she would have preferred some prior warning.

"I thought we could have a chat to begin with and then perhaps we could take a preliminary look around the school to get our bearings," said Mr Harris.

"Of course. Our Vice Principal, Sebastian Swinton, will show you round," said Bethany. "Helga, on your way out, could you ask him to come and see me?"

"Yes, Ms Sedgeford," said Helga. "I'm quite happy to hang on for a while tonight, if you want me to do anything?"

"No, that won't be necessary and what has come over you, Helga?" asked Bethany. She then spoke to the visitors as if Helga wasn't there. "She's usually very punctual about leaving, Dr Sims and Mr Harris. No, I won't be needing you any more tonight; you can get off now."

As Helga left she had the distinct feeling that something had changed in her relationship with her boss. She couldn't put her finger on it but she couldn't stop thinking about how condescending Bethany had been; even more so than usual. It worried her as she was leaving.

Back in the Principal's office, Dr Sims, Mr Harris and Ms Sedgeford, were discussing matters educational. "I'll come straight to the point," said Dr Sims "We may and I stress *may* decide not to have a snap inspection this term, as it's not ideal so late in the academic year but, if that is the case, you can be sure of one soon after."

"Any time is fine by all of us, teachers and pupils alike, at Southgreen," said Bethany.

Sebastian caught Helga coming through the staff room and said, "Have you seen Randy Andy?"

"Can't say I have," replied Helga.

"If you do, tell him I want my CD ROM back tonight, would you?"

"The wicked witch of the west wants to see you immediately," said Helga.

"About?" asked Sebastian.

"Probably nothing important," replied Helga, doing Basil no favours at all.

"It'll be about the fucking timetable again, I bet. Honestly, why does everybody want everything done yesterday, eh Helga? Should be my fucking theme tune." With that Sebastian parted company with the school secretary and started whistling the McCartney classic to cheer himself up. He barged straight into the Principal's office saying, "Helga said it was nothing important boss, but I thought -" but was stopped in his tracks by what he was confronted with.

"Ah, there you are, Sebastian. May I introduce you to Mr Harris and Dr Sims from the inspectorate. I'd like you to show them round." All the blood drained from Sebastian Swinton's face and, for once, he was lost for words.

♦ ♦ ♦

The clock in the staff room now read 17.10 as Andy and Dick returned from their squash match, earlier than Andy had thought, as he'd slaughtered his opponent.

"That's four straight wins," said Andy. "You're just going to have to get some practice in."

"You were a bit lucky in the last game," replied Dick. "Anyway, I broke a string on my racket,"

"A bad workman always blames his tool."

"The first round's on me again, then."

"Not tonight, mate, I'm meeting someone."

"Who now?" said Dick, who couldn't keep up with Andy's sex life, but then Andy could scarcely do that himself!

"Never you mind," he replied.

"You get all the luck. Is there anything you don't win at?"

"Only getting stuck with a boring, self-pitying loser like you," said Andy, but Dick looked crestfallen, so he quickly added, "only joking. We'll have that pint another time."

"Suppose I'll always be your number two."

"You want to watch yourself, mate, or you'll end up like Mr Tambourine Man, in Science. You ought to be applying for a head of department job somewhere else."

"I can't really be bothered. Probably wouldn't get selected even if I did," said Dick, fulfilling Andy's opinion of him as a self-pitying loser.

"The eternal pessimist, eh?" said Andy. "Whereas me; I keep my options open and always look on the bright side. Then nothing can go wrong."

"Can I touch you?"

"Here, steady on!"

"No, I mean perhaps your luck will rub off on me."

"Cheer up, mate," said Andy, "you never know what may fall into your lap." He then offered Dick his hand for a high five and Dick reciprocated, before leaving saying, "Later."

What neither of them had seen nor heard however was that, concealed in the quiet, computer area of the staff room, sat Dave doing some plans, in triplicate, for the following day.

Nor did Andy see him there among the computers, as he poured himself a glass of water from the kitchen area, drank it, and then went to collect his sports bag, just as Julia appeared from nowhere.

"Julia, I thought we agreed we wouldn't meet here, after what happened last week," said Andy.

"Sorry, honey, I was just passing and had this overwhelming urge to -"

"I can't tonight, babe, I've got all these lesson plans to do. Basil gave me the wrong CD ROM."

Julia threw her arms around him saying, "Well, if you're busy later we'll just have to get it out of the way right now!"

Untypically, Andy responded saying, "Julia, I've just had a strenuous game of squash; I can't manage -"

But Julia was having none of that and, giggling, said, "You're not telling me you can't get it up?"

"Of course not," said Andy, instantly realising what a blot on his reputation, as Southgreen's very own stud, this would be; his only real rival being young Mr McGregor, the vet, with his long rubber glove and semen filled syringe.

But Julia was now laughing out loud and ran out of the staff room crying, "Catch me if you can!"

Dave couldn't get enough of what he was witnessing, as the last time he had seen the pair together, Julia was slapping Randy Andy round the face. He distinctly heard Andy, muttering under his breath, "Shit!"

Helga was on her way home but thinking about stopping off at ASDA, and listening to Mick Jagger, who was screaming out a song about wanting to make love, though it was really about wanting to have sex. She didn't know it, because she was pre-occupied with musing about what her boss was up to, and deliberating on what her two teenage daughters would like for their dinner, nevertheless, the song was a soundtrack for what was now going on at Southgreen as Julia let herself into Andy's office, with her oh, so, very, precious key and started to tear off her clothes, leaving behind a trail of red underwear.

She entered the changing area and, divesting herself of her knickers, threw them on the floor, getting straight into the shower and turning on the water. Andy then entered his office and immediately noticed Julia's blouse, skirt and red bra lying on the floor. He grabbed hold of them and, as he passed through to the changing area, he picked up her knickers and held them to his face, savouring and almost salivating on the scent before throwing them down again. Julia had heard him and said, "Little Miss Muffet wants her Grand Old Duke right now!" That was all the encouragement he needed, and kicking off his trainers, he tore off his clothes, threw them on the bench with Julia's stuff and joined her in the shower, closing the swivel door behind him saying, "I'll have to be quick."

"You generally are," giggled Julia.

"And this is positively the last time," said Randy Andy.

"Relax," said Julia.

Meanwhile, Dave was still in the staff room as Sebastian, Mr Harris and Dr Sims entered from the Principal's office. Simultaneously, Françoise came in from the corridor and seeing Dave said, "Have you seen Andy?"

"You just missed him," replied Dave and she turned tail and left.

Sebastian was holding a CD ROM and fidgeting with it. He smiled ingratiatingly at the inspectors saying, "If you don't mind I've got to catch Mr Bailey before he goes home, as I've got the draft timetable for next year on a CD and - bit of a mix up - won't bore you with it, but let's just say that we'll start our guided tour of the great and wonderful educational institution which is Southgreen Academy, down in the nether regions of the PE Department."

As they left, Dave thought for a second, laughed to himself and followed them out, keeping a safe distance.

Back in the red hot shower, Andy hadn't lost his touch, as Julia was telling him, "Yes, like that, Andy; just like that!"

"I know you like that," said Andy.

"Oh, I do, I do! Don't stop, Andy. Don't stop!"

Under her breath, Françoise started to curse the shoe repairer who had cut the key to the door of Andy's office, as she was turning it in the lock but still the door wouldn't open. She pulled it out slightly, wiggled it, tried again and this time she had success. As she entered, she left the door ajar and stopped to listen to the sounds of steaming sex in the shower. She heard Julia moaning, saying,

"Oh, yes! Oh yes, Andy. Yes, yes, yes! Oh, Andy!

The furious Françoise passed silently through the office and came into the changing area. She noticed the clothes on the bench and picked up the red knickers from the floor. She went to spit on them but stopped herself and tore and ripped at them instead, throwing them back down, isolated from the other clothes and towels.

Andy was grunting in an animalistic manner that would have rivalled Mr Bull's young boars and Françoise, even in her fury, still had time for the thought that Andy didn't make noises like that with her and that she certainly wasn't as vocal as Julia, who was arriving at her wet and soapy orgasm, crying, "Oh, my Grand Old

Duke of York! Miss Muffet loves that! Oh, yes, yes, yes, yes, yeeessss!" And after the sibilance and total pleasure of the last letter of that one syllable word, Julia and Andy got a shock that neither of them would ever forget, as the shower door swivelled open and there stood Françoise with a look of murderous intent.

"Oh, no!" said Andy, as Julia screeched in shock. She pushed past Françoise and Andy followed and they both grabbed hold of towels and covered themselves.

Just then, Sebastian and the inspectors, hearing Julia screaming, entered the office.

Françoise slapped Andy round the face saying, "Vous êtes merde!"

Julia said, "You shit, Andy," and slapped the other cheek.

Sebastian, a few paces in front of the inspectors, had witnessed this and entering the changing area, suddenly saw Julia's lonely, red knickers on the floor. He picked them up stealthily and pocketed them, saying, with an improvisational skill that would have rivalled his namesake, Basil, "Just as long as everything's alright then. For a moment I thought we had a problem, what with the screaming and everything. Just high jinks and japes. Well that's okay then. Hunky Dory."

Sweating as profusely as the pigs in the piggery, he then turned to the two bewildered inspectors, following behind and said, "So, Mr Harris and Dr Sims, this is the Unisex Staff Changing area. Not my idea; some of these young things thought it all up. I mean we have now entered the twenty first century, so who are old fogies like us to go against the wishes of the majority? I mean, we do live in a democratic society after all. Though being the son of an old Empire Loyalist, I sometimes rather wish that we didn't!"

"Actually, Mr Swinton, I don't consider myself an old fogey," said Dr Sims

"No, I don't suppose you would," replied Sebastian.

Holding up a map, Mr Harris said, "I thought that this was the Head of PE's office and changing room? That's what it says on this map you've given us."

Sebastian grabbed the map from the Chief Inspector's hand, saying, "Did I give you that one? How stupid of me; way out of date."

Dripping with sweat, Sebastian put his hand into his pocket and, forgetting himself, removed it and mopped his brow with the torn, red knickers he was now holding, saying, "Bloody hot in here. Shall we move on to Modern Foreign Languages? Mademoiselle Poitin (who, at least, was fully clothed) that's your department. Perhaps you'd like to join us?"

But Françoise was still seething, staring at Andy and Julia, both of whom were stood, rigid, covered by towels and fearing for their future. Sebastian steered the inspectors out and turned back to the others saying in a loud whisper, "We need to talk. You all owe me, big time! But, don't worry, I think I might have got away with it!"

Little did any of the actors in this drama know that behind them all, at a safe distance, listening to and spying on them, like a professional voyeur, was Dave Hardman, who chuckled to himself silently, reflecting on the farce that he had just witnessed.

He was still chuckling, now openly, when he arrived back in the staff room, to find Dick Fenwick, sitting alone.

"Quiet tonight," said Dick.

"You could say that. Everybody shot off because of the inspectors."

"Inspectors?" asked Dick, who had not heard the gossip that Helga had started, on her way out, which had emptied the car park in minutes.

"Quick preliminary visit. Not official, of course," said Dave, who was thinking about Sebastian's well-worn phrase about stupidity having its repercussions and also marvelling at the Vice Principal's dexterity in apparently pulling the wool over the inspectors' eyes. Moreover, he now understood exactly what the word 'Vice' meant in his new title.

"I didn't know anything about that," said Dick. "I was playing squash with Andy before and he never mentioned it either."

"Oh, Andy knows all about it, believe you me. In fact he's been keeping them well entertained," said Dave, giving nothing away and picking up his briefcase to make a speedy exit. As he left, Julia rushed past him, crying but Dave didn't stop and made no eye contact. If he had waited a minute however he would have seen that there was, if not another act to the farce he had just been privy to, then at least a postscript, for Julia fell into Dick's arms, sobbing.

"What's the matter?"

"Oh, Dick, it was dreadful."

"What's happened?"

"Me and Andy. We're finished. Finished!"

Dick hugged Julia tightly, and stroked her head, sympathetic to her plight saying, "There, there, you'll be alright. Don't worry, I'll look after you. You don't have to tell me about it if you don't want to but I'm a good listener."

"Oh, thank you, thank you, Dick," said Julia. "I will tell you but not here. Let's go into town. Dick you really are a good friend." Dick was taken aback, as he'd not had much to do with Julia, except in a professional capacity, but was feeling pleased that his concern for her had been acknowledged.

Feeling somewhat safer and out of gratitude more than anything else, Julia held Dick's head between her two hands and kissed his face platonically but repeatedly, her lips pressing against his cheeks and covering his forehead, just as Sebastian entered the staff room accompanied by Mr Harris and Dr Sims, who both looked shocked, yet unsurprised. Sebastian, on the other hand, was ashen faced and turned back through the door almost pushing the inspectors before him, saying, "Oh, I nearly forgot, you haven't seen our new Drama Studio yet, have you? We actually have a professional actor teaching here at the moment. He's been in "The Bill" and everything. He's going for a part in a pot noodles ad on Friday." He stopped short of telling them that young Mr Carter was auditioning for the part of a pornographic film maker, which was just as well, as Mr Harris cut him off saying, "Mr Swinton! I think we've seen quite enough drama for one day!"

Now, at the end of a very short tether, Sebastian replied, "Please yourselves."

♦ ♦ ♦

The staff room clock read 10.00 hours on Tuesday, June 9th. Bethany was sat at her desk, listening in on Helga who was on the phone.

"It must have been, Mr Harris ... oh, I know ... I know ... yes, I know."

Bethany banged her desk in frustration. How could her secretary behave with such disloyalty? She was going to have to do something about it.

"Exactly," said Helga. "Well, you want to see it when there are a lot of things going on at once, don't you? Yes ... yes ...get a true picture ... wait till the autumn?"

Bethany smiled, getting her hopes up.

"No, too far away," continued Helga, "that's what I thought you'd say. Yes ... yes, well, looking at the diary, Tuesday 30th June would be a good day."

Bethany frowned, her hopes of a reprieve now dashed and annoyed with Helga.

"For you too? Good, well we've got the School Council Forum at 11.45 and interviews for the Head of Science job and some year elevens will still be doing their GCSE exams, so you've got a good cross section," said Helga.

Bethany wanted to scream but knew that she had to curtail her anger so, instead, she unlocked a drawer in her desk, removed a packet of cigarettes and lit one, waving away the smoke, while she listened to Helga's voice.

"Did she? She said that she'd heard? No, the door was definitely shut, she likes her privacy ... strange, anyway, you'll be ringing her yourself shortly ...yes ... yes, I will, thanks, Mr Harris."

Helga replaced the receiver but Bethany was enraged. Shaking, she took another large drag on her fag and then stubbed it out on a saucer, shoving it and the cigarettes back into the drawer. She then took some Christian Dior perfume from her handbag, sprayed it on her wrists and neck and then released a few more squirts into the atmosphere which was, to say the least, laced with her own rancour and the smell of stale nicotine, since Bethany hadn't had a cigarette in months and anyway, no one else knew that she smoked.

She called out. "Helga!"

Immediately, Helga entered and said, "What was it you wanted, Ms Sedgeford?"

"Was that Mr Harris you were talking to?" replied Bethany.

"No," said Helga, displaying a mendacity that nonplussed Bethany completely.

"I'm afraid we're going to have to change the date for the interviews for Mr Hill's job; something's come up."

Helga knew that this would scupper Mr Harris's plans and said, "But we can't do that! I've sent out the information packs to the candidates. Anyway, what's come up?"

"I'd forgotten it's a special training day for my position as Justice of the Peace," said Bethany, lying through her teeth, "and I won't be in school on the 30th, so we'll have to cancel the School Council Forum as well."

Without thinking, Helga said, "Very well but he won't like it."

"Who? Who won't like it?" asked Bethany, knowing that she'd caught her out.

"Mr Dylan," Helga replied, recovering her composure. "The other candidates too."

"Well, there's absolutely no way round it. If they want the job they'll just have to be flexible."

There was a momentary truce before Helga asked, "Has Mr Doyle been in here this morning?"

"No, why?"

"I can smell cigarette smoke. He's the only one who would have the blatant nerve to ignore the School Council's 'smoke free' policy."

"Maybe he did pop in here earlier, come to think of it, to inform me about the adult literacy course," said Bethany before Helga offered her some personal advice.

"If you don't mind me saying so, Bethany, I think you've rather overdone it with the perfume today." The Principal remained silent and Helga added, "Anyway, I'd best ring these candidates straight away and put them in the picture." With that, Helga returned to her office, closing the door behind her.

She sat there for a moment, thinking that she'd had enough of Southgreen Academy. Everything had been pleasant under the previous Head, Mr Foulkes. She missed him. They shared a sense of humour and she had always looked forward to coming into school every morning. Now the ambience was decidedly acrid and all she could think about all day was going home to her two daughters, despite their teenage surliness.

She picked up the phone and dialled. "Hello, is it possible to speak to Duncan Lancaster, please ... thanks, yes, it's the school secretary at Southgreen Academy ... I will, yes, thank you."

As she was waiting for Mr Lancaster to come to the phone, Helga reached across her desk and picked up the photograph of her two daughters. She smiled. They'd been so appreciative the night before, as she'd cooked them Coq au vin, which they had loved, saying what a brilliant mother she was. Little did they know it was a ready-made meal from ASDA's new range, but there had been a funny conversation when her thirteen year old had said that, according to her knowledge of French, Coq au vin meant 'Chicken on a lorry.' Helga laughed to herself but her call had now been answered and she said, "Hello there, Mr Lancaster ... yes, it is. I'm terribly sorry but we're going to have to change the date of the interview ... well, I'm glad you're still interested, that's a relief ... I'm sorry I didn't quite get what you were saying there ... I'm afraid I don't know yet but as soon as I do I'll call you ... what was that again? ... Thanks for your patience, Mr Lancaster ... yes, I will, in the next few days. Bye for now."

As Helga put the phone down muttering, "Posh or what?" Bethany smiled because, listening in, she knew that her strategy had worked. She wouldn't have been smiling however if she had known what had happened immediately after the phone call ended because, while Helga was replacing the photo of her beautiful daughters, the base of the frame caught on something. Leaning across her desk and investigating, she discovered the tiny microphone attached to the thin, black wire. She felt the wire and traced its course down the desk leg to the carpet. She knelt down and saw how the wire was concealed underneath and pulled an inch or two of the carpet away, to reveal that it ran along the seam and was secured with double sided tape. She followed the seam of the carpet, like the explorer, Livingstone looking for the source of the

Nile, and when she got to Bethany's door, she pulled another inch or two away. There she saw the wire, which evidently passed underneath the door frame and into Bethany's office. She had the Principal bang to rights. Her mind raced. She knew that with this piece of information, she was now untouchable.

◆ ◆ ◆

It was break time. Randy Andy's reputation had always gone before him and he had led a charmed life at Southgreen but, after the previous afternoon's events, he was left with only one friend in the world. That friend was Mr Hill who, as usual, was fast asleep in his chair but was appearing, to the isolated Head of PE at least, to be offering him a cheeselet. Andy took one from the packet held in the outstretched but motionless hand of the Head of Science and said, "Thanks Hilly Billy" (Andy's personal nickname for him) in the hope that Mr Hill would respond with something like, 'Have another' or
'My pleasure,' but he didn't. Had he responded Andy hoped that he would listen while he unburdened himself of the terrible situation that he now found himself in, being dumped by three women in the course of a week, one of whom was pregnant with his child. Not to mention the undeniable fact that he had been caught having intercourse in the shower with one of the women by one of the other women, and then been found covering his genitalia with a towel, as two school inspectors were being given a tour of the establishment. Sebastian had indeed managed to persuade the gullible inspectors that this unisex changing area was all in order but he had given Andy the most vicious bollocking, bollocking being the appropriate word, after what he'd seen moments before the

inspectors had followed on behind him. Sebastian had been rather shocked by the large size of the offending appendage and accoutrements, and had told Randy Andy that at least he merited his 'fucking nickname.' That was the only comfort that Andy's equally swollen, but now battered ego could gain from the situation, as Françoise entered the staff room, ignoring him and Sebastian did the same. All that was left was for Andy to take another cheeselet from Hilly Billy's packet and let out an audible sigh.

Over in another corner of the staff room sat Tom and Dave. They were joined by Françoise, who hadn't met Tom, though she was to become fascinated after listening to him describing what had just happened in the Drama Studio.

"So, Peter Sutcliffe tells Carl that he can't possibly play both parts: Hitler killing the dog and then committing suicide with Eva Braun and also Goebbels killing his children and then committing suicide with Mrs. Goebbels. Even Carl had to give way on that score and agreed he'd stick to just playing Hitler. Then Miriam Stiff said that she'd like to play Eva Braun, which then stirred Maxine Dalton into saying that Miriam Stiff fancied Carl. Anyway, Peter, very assertively took control of the situation, told them all to shut up and asked if Ricky Knapp, flushed with the success of his supporting role as Hermann, the dog, would like to play Goebbels? Carl agreed that Ricky was small and Goebbels was too and, even though Ricky didn't have a club foot he could limp a bit, but Carl insisted that they re-enact yesterday's scene and that he still wanted Ricky to play Hermann."

"Goebbels or Goring?" asked Dave.

"Neither; the dog, stupid," said Tom, continuing, "anyway, Ricky agreed but said he'd done some homework on the internet and found that Hitler's dog was actually called Blondie. This really got Carl mad and he refused to do the scene again unless he could shoot the dog and still call him Hermann. He said that, after yesterday, it was the only name he could accept while imagining, at the same time, that Ricky was his own dog, Terry."

"I'm confused," said Françoise.

"Not surprised," quipped Dave but Tom continued.

"Anyway, there was then nearly a fight because Peter Sutcliffe made the mistake of, jokingly, saying that he thought Carl should seek psychiatric help, but then Maxine Dalton distracted Carl from punching Peter by saying that it would be weird to have two Hermanns played by the same actor, especially since one of them was a dog. Then Carl said he thought that Maxine was actually right and therefore he would try calling the dog Blondie and Peter suggested that they stop arguing and do the tragic death scene of Goebbels' children first."

"So, they still didn't know that Goebbels was called Joseph not Hermann?" asked Dave.

"No," said Tom, "Ricky's research hadn't stretched further than the dog. Well, Peter was completely organised and roped in some of the others to play the little ones, though there were only four and not six of them. Then Ricky and Maxine started to wind the children up by saying that they had some lovely, sweet, fruity, bedtime drinks for them and, if they were very good and lay down, they could all have one. And Ricky and Maxine were brilliant acting their parts, because they were being very cheerful with the little ones and, at the same time, you could see how upset they really were. And Peter was encouraging the children to beg their parents for the drinks and, eventually Ricky said to them, 'now all lay down quite still because daddy and mummy know what's best,' and the children lay down and they gave them the fruity drinks and as they gradually became motionless, Maxine and Ricky both cried and then, in unison, took their pills and died. And then there was silence, except for the sound of Carl Bormann sobbing uncontrollably."

"This isn't drama, it's therapy," said Dave.

"Anyway," continued Tom, "Carl was so moved by what he had witnessed that he broke down completely and said that he really hated the Nazis now and that the only part he wanted to play was the soldier who had burnt Hitler's body. And Peter said, 'Great Carl, just do it. Get up and do it!' "

"And Carl jumped up and improvised the burning of Hitler's body with total empathy (he said later, 'It was just like torching a car') and they all cheered him and then he asked the group if they could do something else next week and Peter suggested that they improvise guillotining the aristocrats during the French Revolution and everybody said that they thought that sounded cool, and Peter said, 'Yeah, cool and pretty bloody messy!' "

"So that's next week sorted then," said Dave. "You two haven't been properly introduced. Françoise, this is Tom Carter, our temporary drama teacher."

♦ ♦ ♦

Later in the Principal's office, Bethany and Helga were rearranging the dates for the interviews. "So what possible days are there, Helga?" asked Bethany.

"I've narrowed it down to the fourteenth or sixteenth of July."

"Both cutting it fine but I suppose it will have to be the fourteenth," said Bethany.

"And the School Council Forum?"

"It had better be the same."

"Right. I've got those calls to make and then I'll type up the formal letters to the three candidates," said Helga, who then returned to her office and settled down at her desk. She had a mischievous smile on her face in anticipation of what she was going to do next, knowing that Bethany would be listening in. Of course Helga had worked out that the mic could only pick up her voice, as it wasn't connected to the phone. She leant across the desk and spoke closely into the microphone,

"Hello, Mr Harris," she said, to the imaginary inspector. Bethany recoiled from the loud volume and fiddled with the control.

"Yes," said Helga into the mic, "yes, I see ... no, well I can see your point of view ... dreadful shenanigans, yes, but ... not easy ... pointing the finger ... yes, yes, I see, so there won't be an inspection at all this term." A broad smile of sheer relief appeared on Bethany's face but was matched by the smile on Helga's, as she silently applauded her perfect performance.

"No, it's not an ideal time, Mr Harris," said Helga, purely for the Principal's benefit. "I understand ... next term yes ... but not immediately." Bethany was now chuckling to herself; things always had a way of working out, she thought.

"No, you can count on me," continued Helga, trying to get the pauses right so that it seemed as if she actually was talking to Mr Harris. "I won't tell her ... yes, yes, keeps them ... on their ... yes, toes, yes ...exactly Mr Harris. You'll speak to her yourself, yes. Will you, won't you? Yes. Good idea. Keep her guessing ... alright, I will ... no ... yes ... Lanzarotte actually ... have you? Is it? Volcanic, yes ... nude beaches? We should send a few of our teachers there then, eh, Mr Harris? ... I will ... and you. Bye then." Helga then lifted the phone receiver, quietly, and then replaced it loudly for effect. She was delighted by her acting and particularly with the reference to the summer holiday, which was inspired.

Bethany opened the adjoining door and stood in the doorway, grinning.

"What are you looking so cheerful about?" asked Helga.

"Actually, I was just thinking about the tennis at Wimbledon. I'm looking forward to it, Helga. I do love the total, uninterrupted coverage of the fortnight. It's one of the delights of British life. With nothing else to distract you, you can immerse yourself totally in the atmosphere."

"I can't see what all the fuss is about. Generally, I fall asleep when the tennis is on. I used to fancy Pat Cash though."

At that moment, the phone rang and Helga answered. "Hello ... yes, she is. I'll just put you through." Helga turned to Bethany and said, "It's Mr Harris for you."

Bethany returned to her office and picked up the phone, having a short conversation with the real inspector, who was rather perturbed by what he and Dr Sims had seen the previous day but had accepted Sebastian's explanation and was still dithering about whether there would be an inspection in the summer term. Bethany of course, was rather impressed by his performance, for that is what she thought it was, though Mr Harris had no idea yet about the bugging.

Later on Helga was gathering her things to go home when Bethany entered and said, "Did you manage to contact the candidates?"

"Yes and I got the letters off. I've left one for Mr Dylan in his pigeon hole."

"Could you put these jobs newsletters in the staff room, on your way out, Helga, please?"

"Certainly."

"You ought to have a look, Helga. You'd be amazed at the number of secretarial positions that are available in local schools."

"I'm not looking."

"No, I don't suppose you would be at your age," said Bethany, who was under the misguided illusion that she now held the upper hand over her secretary. The Principal returned to her desk, where she took from her locked drawer a bottle of scotch and poured herself a large celebratory glass.

Helga took the newsletters and put them on the tables in the staff room, unperturbed by Bethany's barbed comment. She knew that knowledge was power and the dirt she had on Bethany's bugging activity put her in the driving seat, even if she was feeling abused and isolated.

Just after Helga had left an empty staff room, Linda Baker, the pregnant, depressed Head of Maths entered, clutching a small photograph. She crossed to the photocopier and put the photo on the glass. She pressed some buttons to enlarge the photo to A4 size and, when that was successful, she removed the original from the glass. She opened the lower drawer and removed a piece of A4 paper which she then wrote on with a bright red board marker. Then she pinned the enlarged photo and the piece of paper she'd written on, to the middle of the staff notice board and left as quickly as she had arrived.

A minute later Sebastian and Dave both appeared and the Vice Principal crossed to look at the notice board.

"Your bastard child, Andy" said Sebastian, reading the piece of paper with the red writing on.

"Nothing to do with me, mate," said Dave.

"Not yours, Andy's," said Sebastian. "She's only gone and stuck a blown up photo of her scan on the notice board. This'll be good craic in the morning!"

Dave crossed over to look at the photo and said, "Is it a boy or a girl?"

They both craned their heads to get a comprehensive view of the scan and the Sebastian answered saying, "Can't really tell," and pointing to something protruding said, "What's that?"

"Oh, that's from the ink on the photocopying glass," Dave replied. "The blob comes up on everything at the moment but it's blown up eight times the size here."

"I was going to say he takes after his father," said Sebastian.

"How would you know?" asked Dave only to be confronted with Sebastian giving him the beady eye of incredulity.

"Sorry Seb," said Dave. "I forgot what you'd seen for a moment."

"I wish I could fucking forget," said Sebastian, looking again at the scan again and saying, "Bloody amazing, isn't it?"

"Yes," said Dave, "every life a universe."

"Sorry?"

"Well the sperm and the egg are infinitesimally small, invisible to the naked eye, yet from this nothing comes a person."

"Incredible. I never knew."

"Which is just like the way that all the matter in the universe started as this incredibly dense, infinitesimally small piece of nothing and ended in everything we can see on a starlit night. So, every life a universe."

"Profound," said Sebastian, "except it's total fucking bollocks!"

"How do you know?"

"Because, my dear professor, your analogy would work if it wasn't for one small thing."

"And what, I pray, is that?"

"Well, as you so rightly say, you get this conglomeration of cells that double and multiply and develop into a foetus and grow limbs and eyes and hearts and minds, in the wonderfully safe and nurturing environment of the womb, and then emerge to become a sweet, little, goo goo dribbling, bubble blowing baby, who grows up to be ... Carl Borman!"

Dave took a second to consider this and said, "You're right." Then they both took another second and said, in unison, "Total fucking bollocks!"

And while the two stalwarts of Southgreen Academy were philosophising about the existential nature of life and the universe, another stalwart of the said institution, namely Helga was on her mobile phone. "Hello, Mr Harris," she said, "can you hear me? Am I breaking up? That okay? Where? ... No, I'm not at school ... no, I'm in the car park at ASDA. You'll have to call me on this number in future ... She knows we've been talking, Mr Harris ... I found a tiny microphone secreted on my desk ... yes, she's been bugging me! ... Outrageous, yes ... yes ... resignation, yes ... if I made a formal complaint ... I will think about it ... I think she wants to sack me but she's bitten off ... exactly ... I won't, Mr Harris don't you worry. She doesn't frighten me!"

◆ ◆ ◆

The next morning, Helga was listening to Radio One as she drove into work, safe in the knowledge that she wasn't as isolated as she had felt, as the dithering but charming Mr Harris knew exactly what sort of pressure she was under. She was enjoying the sixties hour, as the DJ had played several Rolling Stones songs but the track playing as she pulled into the car park at Southgreen was a song by The Strawbs about being in a trade union. This gave her courage as she prepared to face the day ahead and whatever her superior had to throw at her for, in her dreams, Bethany had presented her with a P45.

As she was hanging up her coat, Sebastian knocked and entered, saying, "Morning Helga."

"Morning Seb," she replied.

Sebastian knocked on the adjoining door to Bethany's office and entered, saying, "Morning boss."

Bethany did not answer but carried on reading her paper and then, after a few seconds she said, "Sebastian, I'm afraid I won't be able to take my double Year 10 history today, periods one and two."

"And why might that be?"

"Something of a rather personal nature," said Bethany, not looking up from her tabloid.

"Women's problems, boss?"

"How very sensitive, Seb."

"And has this been on the cards for long or has it just cropped up at 8.20 when I've already done the cover list?" said Sebastian, but Bethany didn't look up.

"Funnily enough there's a scan photo of Linda and Andy's nipper on the notice board with a sign saying, 'your bastard child, Andy,' so women's problems seem to be pretty high on the agenda this morning!" said Sebastian.

"You seem a bit agitated, Sebastian."

"That's okay, don't you worry about me. "You just relax and read that great organ of unfettered liberalism, The Daily Mail."

"You're behind the times, Sebastian," said Bethany, finally looking up. "Even Mail readers are Blairites now."

"God help us," said Sebastian "and I never thought I'd hear myself say this but bring back Arthur Scargill. He said it like it was and told the bloody truth!"

"You're entitled to your opinion, Sebastian," said Bethany and indeed he was.

Sebastian, might have been a picture of horrid harassment, both given and received but, like so many others, he didn't like governments interfering unnecessarily in education. He and Dave, whom Sebastian regarded as a full blown, card carrying member of the revolution, were both in agreement on this. Southgreen had become one of the first academy schools and Bethany Sedgeford was probably destined for super-head status in her bid to turn it round, but he could only see it as a slippery slope, where more influence would eventually be given to outside, private interests, with their own agendas, which laid the door wide open to corruption, and more absolute power would be invested in whomever was the government Education Minister at the time. The drive for better results would only lead to massaging the figures and manipulating outcomes by fair means or foul and, whatever way you viewed it, would only mean more years of jumping through hoops, with daft changes in the curriculum, creating more unnecessary work for an overworked and under-valued staff, most of whom were heading for an early breakdown or cardiac arrest and who just wished the politicians would all fuck off.

Of course, Dave was of the opinion that nothing would ever change in society until the playing fields of Eton and Harrow were given over to the local communities, and that the idea that rich people could pay for a superior education became an anathema, in the same way that equal access to healthcare had now been accepted by most British people as being a fundamental human right. But, as Sebastian was letting these thoughts gather, as the Principal read her copy of the Daily Mail, he was also blissfully unaware that, for so many reasons, he was also part of the problem.

Snapping out of his momentary reverie he said, "Well, have you got it?"

"Got what?" asked Bethany.

"Your lesson plan in triplicate, with learning objectives and teaching activities, for the department and for the inspectorate and one for yourself? Or should I say for the poor supply teacher, most likely Mr Carter, who happens to be on stand-by, periods one and two. On pain of a slow death? Or is that just for the poor minions who actually happen to teach more than two lessons a week?"

"I haven't had time," said Bethany. "It was a last minute thing."

"It is supposed to be *pre*-planning but fine! Well, perhaps you could provide at least an idea for Mr Carter about what he should be teaching? I mean, what is it that these inquisitive young minds are studying at the moment?" asked Sebastian.

"The French Revolution," replied the errant Principal.

"Well might I suggest that you send down for the guillotine from the art department and they can practise cutting off each other's heads. Perhaps they could start with fingers and work their way up!"

"Don't be ridiculous, Sebastian, they can watch the video with that man; you know, the one who does the history programmes."

"Would that be A.J.P. Taylor?"

"No, it would not!" snapped Bethany. "It's on the shelf at the back of the classroom. Channel Six on the television. The children can take notes. Learning objective: to understand the French Revolution! Sebastian, you really ought to chill out."

Now, Sebastian was incensed. "Chill out? Chill out! I mean what is the world coming to? Not 48 hours ago, I lead two inspectors to the PE Department, on your instructions, where they very nearly witness what was probably a sordid orgy of sex and God knows what else, and returning to the staff room some twenty minutes later they find the same woman they'd seen almost naked, covered only by a towel, in all likelihood post coitally, now repeatedly kissing a different member of staff and you say 'chill out'! "

"Yes, well, first, Julia Lyons is not on the staff and there were no children on the premises at that late hour and secondly, I've talked to Mr Bailey about his inappropriate behaviour and he's been warned severely but I also have some important inside information," said Bethany, ready to drop the bombshell. She paused for a beat and then said "We won't be having an inspection this term."

Completely taken aback Sebastian said, "Sorry? You mean ... oh, thank you, thank you, thank you!" With those words the Vice Principal knelt before his superior, as if he was about to make a proposal of marriage and said, "There is a God and she's a woman named Bethany Sedgeford!"

"Oh, don't go overboard, Sebastian."

"When did you hear?" asked Sebastian, rising.

"Let's just say," said the Principal, "that I have it on good authority. So, if you wouldn't mind telling them at the briefing, that they can all relax and throw away those silly lesson plans till next term. We're going to have a nice, calm, tranquil summer."

Forgetting himself, Sebastian replied, "Fucking brilliant!"

"I couldn't agree more," said Bethany, as she was grabbed hold of and hugged by her number two.

♦ ♦ ♦

At the mid-morning break Andy was sitting next to Mr Hill again. He offered the narcoleptic Head of Science a chocolate Penguin but there was no response. Hilly Billy's outstretched hand was clutching an open packet of Cheeselets, so Andy took one. Françoise entered and Andy rose to try and greet her but she ignored him. Sebastian entered, holding a small cucumber in his hand and Andy rose again but received the same treatment. He slumped back in his chair, disconsolate, then removed from his pocket the scan photo of his future child. He tried to show it to Mr

Hill and, even though he was motionless, Andy still entered into a one sided conversation.

"Look, you can see its little spine," said Andy, pointing, "and that's not what you think it is; it's just an ink blob on the photocopying glass. They didn't tell her the sex."

Sebastian then collared Tom and said, "So, Mr Carter, how did you get on with Year 10 history?"

"Well, the video didn't last long, so I was a bit stuck really, because of the lack of a plan."

"I'm so sorry about that," said Sebastian. "There seems to be one rule for mere mortals like us and another for our God like leader."

"Peter Sutcliffe, Carl Borman and Miriam Stiff asked if they could dramatise some of the scenes," said Tom, "so they did Louis and Marie Antoinette's flight to Varenne, followed by the storming of the Bastille, guillotining the aristocrats and Charlotte Corday stabbing Marat in the bath."

"Funny, it always comes down to serial murder with our young Sutcliffe, doesn't it? Well, can't stand here chatting all day, the timetable beckons. If I don't see you before, good luck on Friday or should I say, 'break a leg.' "

"Sorry?" said Tom, being a bit slow on the uptake.

"Pot noodles? Pornographic film maker?" said Sebastian. "If you want to rehearse it, I'm sure Mademoiselle Poitin here would help. After what I saw the other day, I think she could manage dripping hot noodles down her—"

But Sebastian was saved from finishing his improper break time banter by Dave who said, "Talking of which, why are you holding a cucumber?"

"Ah, nearly forgot. It's for you, Mr Dylan. The very same Peter Sutcliffe thrust it into my hand before I could tell him to bugger off, and said could I let you have it?"

Françoise and Dave both laughed.

"God, you've got dirty minds," said Sebastian turning to Mr Dylan. "Something to do with his old grandfather, who's disabled."

"Yes, and is also called Peter, apparently," said Mr Dylan.

"I was right," said Dave quietly, remembering his conversation on the first day of term with Mr Bull.

"Quite a few weeks ago," continued Mr Tambourine Man, "he was going on and on at me, you know how he does, about his old granddad being crippled with arthritis, in a wheelchair now, and not being able to cultivate his prize cucumbers for the village flower show. So, he asked me if he could use one of the old greenhouses on the disused allotments, so that he could grow them as a surprise for him."

"Did he indeed? Well this specimen is first of the early crop," said Sebastian, handing the green phallus to Mr Dylan. "You may do with it what you will."

"Peter might be a prize pillock but he's got some initiative, I'll give him that," said Mr Dylan.

"I'll say," agreed Tom.

Checking to see that Mr Hill was still asleep but lowering his voice in case he was only dozing and could hear, Mr Dylan said, "You should see Peter's plans for 'sparkler,' " touching his nose. "He's really taken to designing some interesting rockets and pyrotechnics for the summer fair." Then, finishing his coffee, he bid them farewell saying, "Well, time and tide as they say."

"Who do?" asked Dave, mischievously.

"They do," replied Mr Dylan, boringly. "Did I tell you that the date for the interview has been changed to the fourteenth? Prolongs the agony but gives me more time to practise any questions that the panel might throw at me."

"No, you didn't tell me," replied Dave, "but now that you have, you'd better run along and start practising."

"I'd better had," said Mr Dylan and when he was out of earshot Dave said,

"Who gets your vote for top prize pillock?"

Pointing at Mr Dylan, Tom started to sing the famous song, that had spawned the science teacher's nickname, and Françoise joined in. They both then laughed, pointing at the Head of Science, as the listener in the classic hit was wide awake and nowhere near as sleepy as the narcoleptic Mr Hill, who was flat out now and snoring!

Then Françoise said to Dave, "I had a word with Mr Latham."

"And?"

"He says there's not a problem about posing for Peter's GCSE art project as long as he's around in the art department to supervise. Peter can use the 'A' Level studio. It's quiet there and will be empty after the sixth form exams"

"Does Peter know?"

"Yes," said Françoise. "We talked about it. He says he wants to reconstruct one of Goya's famous 'Maja' paintings."

"The woman on the chaise longue?" asked Dave.

"Yes," said Françoise. "I told him that I was willing to pose for the clothed Maja but not the naked one."

Together, Dave and Tom said, "Spoilsport."

After the break, in the Principal's office Bethany was talking to Mr Harris on the phone, while Sebastian watched on, though she was far more interested in the article she was reading in OK! magazine about Venus Williams. Still, she pretended to be paying attention to the inspector. "Yes, Mr Harris, yes, I know," she said. "Yes, I understand, yes, yes … well, yes, of course, we're ready whenever you want to … no … yes, I know, yes … can't … yes, be sure … yes, Mr Harris."

At this point Bethany yawned in an exaggerated manner and Sebastian responded by holding up his fist and punching his other hand, before returning to his other pre-occupation which was studying a printout of the draft timetable.

"Yes, Mr Harris, well you'll get back to me then ... yes, don't know when ... yes, exactly, Mr Harris ... yes, well, till then, then ... yes, bye, Mr Harris, bye." As soon as she had replaced the receiver she said, "Dickhead!"

This got Sebastian's immediate attention and he looked up from the timetable saying, "What did you say?"

"I'm sorry, Seb I must be catching it from someone but he really does keep going on and on about possible surprise visits, when I know it's all absolute nonsense."

"How do you know, boss?" asked Sebastian.

"I just do, Seb. That's why I'm the Principal and you're my deputy."

"Of course, boss," said Sebastian, subserviently, immediately becoming engrossed in his timetable again.

"And together, Seb, we can make a difference; no we will make a difference," said Bethany with authority.

Hardly listening Sebastian said, "Absolutely, boss. Couldn't agree more. Together, we'll ... be different and ... you know ... do whatever it is you just said we'd do."

♦ ♦ ♦

It was Tom's round at the Royal Oak at lunchtime, on the following Monday.

"Your pint, Dave; Françoise, your wine," he said as he took the drinks from the tray and placed them in front of his colleagues.

"I shouldn't but thanks," said Françoise.

"So, how did the pot noodles audition go then?" asked Dave.

"Steamy," said Tom.

"Don't ring us we'll –"

"No, but I haven't heard yet," said Tom. "There were only forty actors up for the part."

"It must be a very frustrating business," said Françoise, sympathetically.

"It can be," replied Tom. "So, who've you got this afternoon, then?"

"I'm free period five and Peter Sutcliffe has art then, so we're doing another session."

"How is the aspiring Goya?" asked Dave.

"He won't let me see what he's done yet," said Françoise. "He's very quiet. Just concentrates and observes but hardly says a word. If I glimpse him though, behind his easel, sometimes I can almost tell what he's thinking."

"He was on top form in drama, this morning," said Tom. "They've started this massive improvisation that Peter, aided by the reformed Carl Borman, has persuaded the whole group to attempt. After the French Revolution stuff, the other day, Peter told them the story of Che Guevara and Fidel Castro's heroic overthrow of the Cuban dictator, Batista. Today, Carl was wearing a non-school uniform beret and a bandana."

"What else is he planning?" asked Françoise.

"Well, Peter has this way of distracting them," said Tom, "so that he changes his mind and they do too, almost without realising that they've done it."

"Charismatic, eh?" said Dave.

"So, now he's persuaded them that what they really ought to be doing, is an in depth exposé of scientific research on animals and he's, quite subtly, trying to rope in support for his School Council proposal to close the farm, as well."

"Wow," said Dave.

"And he brought in some horrific images of terrible animal slaughter to show the group and Carl said, if anyone did that to his Terry he'd blow them across the Bay of Pigs with his dad's twelve bore."

"So, Carl's just one step behind," said Dave.

"Yes," said Tom, "Peter's loyal and trusty henchman. Miriam and Maxine are also heavily involved now, and Ricky Knapp tags along too."

Françoise raised her glass proposing a toast, saying, "Here's to the sans-culottes, better known at Southgreen as the revolutionary council of SALAMI."

Altogether they exclaimed, "SALAMI!" raising and clinking glasses in approval.

♦ ♦ ♦

A week later at the morning briefing, Bethany was coming to the end of her daily pep talk.

"And may I remind you," she said, "that the staff do will be on the evening of Monday, July 13th. I know Monday's not the best day for a party of this nature, but at least it gives everyone the rest of the week to recover. It's eighteen pounds per head and will be held, as usual, at the French Bistro in the High Street."

"If I might add," said Sebastian, "that a list is already up on the notice board and I should say that the price does include wine, with the meal, but not aperitifs and the gallons of alcohol you'll probably consume afterwards. Also, I would remind Mr Dylan that he has rather an important interview the following day, so he'd better just stick to mineral water. Mr Hill, on the other hand has no excuse than to get absolutely pissed as a fart, eh, Mr Hill?"

Almost used to his swearing by now, still Bethany chastised him, saying, "Sebastian!"

Mr Hill did not answer so Sebastian added, "Please yourself."

"Anything else from anybody?" said Bethany, noticing that Susan Shepherd was trying to get her words out but couldn't and, even if she had been able to, was interrupted by Sebastian saying, "If I may continue, boss. Just to keep you all up to date on Mr Carter's celebrity status, unfortunately he didn't get the pot noodles ad; apparently they chose a Peter Stringfellow look-alike instead. He is however auditioning for a public information film on Thursday and so will not be in school. What's the film about, Mr Carter?"

Tom, now used to his new found status, replied, "Children not accepting sweets from strangers. It's part of the 'Stranger Danger' campaign."

"And don't tell me," said Sebastian, "you're up for the part of the stranger?"

"Yes," said Tom.

"It's an interesting niche you're falling into, casting wise, Mr Carter but if I were you, I'd have a quiet word with your agent."

Everybody laughed.

"Are we all done then?" asked Bethany. "Anything else? Support staff? Susan?"

Susan was now straining to speak but the words came out in such a high pitched tone that, as usual, no one could understand.

"Oh, Susan, do spit it out, you're amongst friends here," said Bethany.

With monumental effort, Susan did spit the words out but very quietly and quickly indeed, saying, "Can we bring partners?"

"What did she say," asked Bethany, who was some distance away.

Françoise came to her aid however and said, "She says, can we bring partners to the staff do?"

"I didn't know you had a partner, Susan," said Bethany. "Yes, of course you can bring him, what's his name?"

Susan's face went as red as an indelible board marker as she blurted out, much louder now, "Angela." Everybody took a moment to digest this information before Bethany said, "How very progressive. Yes, do bring Angela, Susan. And are we to expect one of these new civil partnerships in the near future?"

But this was too much for Susan, who shook her head in total panic, rather than as if she were saying 'no.'

"No?" said Bethany. "Well I'm so thrilled, Susan, that you've chosen this particular forum to come out in. You're always guaranteed of our support, you know that. You do a wonderful job!"

There was applause all round and Susan was literally beside herself, in a frenzy of both pride and indecision, as she hadn't intended to come out at all! Though she could not control herself, at least to some extent, unintentionally, she had taken control.

"Have a nice day, everyone," said Bethany, bringing the briefing to a close.

♦ ♦ ♦

Over a week later, Peter had something to be happy about. His granddad, aka Peter, had bought him something, for his fifteenth birthday, which he had treasured from the very moment that he had ripped open the wrapping paper. It was an iPod. It had room for at least a thousand songs. The song that was playing now was, appropriately, the Dylan song about an artist and his masterpiece. The singer might have had an assignation with a young female relative of the artist, Botticelli, but now Peter was painting his portrait of Goya's clothed Maja, with Françoise Poitin, as the almost identical model.

For the French teacher had gone to great lengths to look as near to the original as she could. She was wearing a long, voluminous white dress, with a sown-in pink sash under her breasts and a gold and black blouse draped around her shoulders. Her jet black hair, opposed by her pink cheeks and shining, cherry red lips were almost indistinguishable from the original Goya model but now, in the first decade of the twenty first century, Françoise was an inspiration to another male artist of undoubted talent.

"So, how are your granddad's cucumber's coming on, Peter?" asked Françoise.

But in Peter's ear the only words that he could hear were Bob Dylan's, singing about moving rapidly, in an elevated location, towards a flock of wild geese. This sparked off a strange and eerie premonition, which made him mess up his brush stroke. He tutted, picking up a cloth and that was the sum total of his reply.

"Peter, I know you have to concentrate very hard but a little conversation would be in order, I'm sure. Mr Dylan told me the other day that you are making fireworks for the summer fair that will spell Mr Hill's name in the sky ... that's very impressive, Peter."

But Peter hadn't mentioned his concealed iPod, as it was against school rules to have one, and the only words now ringing in his ears were about the song's protagonist, arriving by plane in the capital of Belgium, where young girls were so keen on clamouring to get a glimpse of the artist, that they were incurring severe muscular strains; an image that Peter was trying to conceptualise.

"I have framed the drawing you did of me as a mermaid. It's beside the poem and takes pride of place on my mantelpiece," said Françoise.

But again Peter didn't answer, as Dylan was now, circumnavigating the world in a grubby, Venetian punt, while wishing for his return to the country that gave us all Coca-Cola. This sparked off a craving for sugar in the young artist and he decided it was time for a break and a coke in the canteen.

"Peter, this painting seems to be taking more sessions than you said. I mean, I know you want to get it right but I hope you're not spinning it out?"

Peter couldn't hear any of this as, while he was completing the final brush strokes of the day, the inspirational Dylan lyrics were implanting the sincere hope that, in the realisation of his ambitious plans, everything was going to run as smoothly as one of Franz Liszt's great Hungarian compositions, which he'd also been listening to in recent days.

Françoise however thought that she'd offended him when he got up, left his easel and headed for the canteen.

"I'm sorry," said Françoise. "That's not fair. I know how seriously you take your work. I know you're not spinning it out, Peter. Please forgive me ... I'm really sorry. Say that you'll forgive me, Peter!"

But Peter had gone.

♦ ♦ ♦

It was now midday and Bethany was on the phone as Sebastian entered saying, "If I might have another word about the draft timetable, boss, would you mind being first cover, period one, every other Thursday?"

"Yes, yes, I know, Mr Harris," said Bethany, covering the mouthpiece and whispering, "Sorry, Seb, it's him again."

"Dickhead," said Sebastian.

Still covering the mouthpiece Bethany said, "No, double dickhead," and they both shared a wicked laugh. "No," said Bethany, "time's getting on, I know ... yes, the twenty first, that's right. So, there's not long left now ... yes, Mr Harris, I get the picture ... yes, I know, you never know ... well we're all prepared here, whenever it is."

If Helga could have heard the conversation she would have been delighted, as Mr Harris was playing his part to perfection, but Helga was at the photocopier, chatting to Mr Dylan, who was wearing his yellow hard hat again and carrying a large box. "I spoke to Mr Lancaster again today," she said.

"Really, Helga?"

"Yes, a quiet man but beautifully spoken, though I have to say, his accent was so posh I had trouble understanding him. Of course, that's what you get from an Oxbridge education, I suppose."

"Silver spoon syndrome, I think you call it. Still, I'd better get this lot down to the science lab PDQ."

"What's in it?"

"Special ingredients for the pyrotechnic display."

"That's certainly a feather in your cap."

"Yes, I'm hoping it will go in my favour, come the big day."

"I'm sure it will but you've got stiff opposition. Mr Warwick, the other candidate, has a first class degree from Jesus College, Cambridge."

"You're depressing me now, Helga. What chance have I got when he's got God on his side?"

Helga started to laugh. She was a bit of an expert on sixties' music.

"What's so funny?"

"Well, it's just ... the song, silly ...you know by Bob Dylan, Mr Dylan. It's about having God on his side."

"Why does everybody make jokes about my name," said Mr Dylan in frustration, as he left, struggling to get the large box through the staff room door.

♦ ♦ ♦

A week later, on the day of the staff do, Françoise, Tom and Dave were having, what had now become, their daily, lunchtime drink at The Royal Oak, when through the door walked Julia and Dick.

"Do you see what I see?" asked Dave.

"Yes, I do," replied Françoise.

Julia and Dick waved politely and Tom and Dave reciprocated. Françoise, on the other hand, moved her chair so that she didn't have to look at Julia saying, "The view is much better this way."

"So, when do you do the 'Stranger Danger' film?" asked Dave.

"Straight after the end of term. It couldn't be better. And I've been offered a part in the theatre."

"Where's that?" asked Françoise.

"Dundee Rep."

"In Scotland?"

"Yes," said Tom, "I'll be up there for a couple of months."

"So, how's the animal rights improvisation coming on?" asked Dave.

"It's their assessment tomorrow," said Tom. "The head of Year 10 has agreed that some other students can come and watch. If you're free periods one and two, you're very welcome. They've cottoned on to the idea, through doing the Goebbels' family suicide impro, that children in danger makes very good drama, so the plot is about the kidnap of an animal researcher's two young children. Peter has really galvanised them into action."

"And how's his masterpiece coming on, Françoise?" asked Dave.

"Well, he says that he's nearly finished but he said that two weeks ago. We're having another session, period three tomorrow," said Françoise.

"I wish there were more teachers like you two. It gives me faith in the future."

"How do you mean?" asked Tom.

"Well, you've got energy, enthusiasm and idealism running through your veins and the children definitely respond to it. I mean just look at the development in, say, Carl Borman and Ricky Knapp since you've been teaching them drama, Tom. So many teachers start out with the same aspirations but the drudgery and bureaucracy disillusions them and they become another cog in the machine, which churns out results and, we're told, improves standards. Consequently, young teachers are leaving in droves and it's going to get worse. The thing is we're not improving standards for the benefit of the children, we're doing it for the self-aggrandisement of the politicians. And it's been the same since the sixties. Once comprehensive education had been won and broadly accepted as the way forward, the whole argument became about whether private education should be abolished because it was unfair and perpetuated the class system. But if you stood up and suggested that today, at any party political conference, you'd get shouted down and, probably, forcefully ejected from the hall!"

"There's still selection too, whatever they say," said Tom.

"Yes, we still have it here," said Dave. The point is that the system can never be truly comprehensive, while private schools and grammars still exist. The politicians try to deny it with talk of choice and meritocracy, but while the Home Office and our embassies around the world are mainly full of people who went to Eton or Harrow or any of the other bastions of privilege, there can be no meritocracy; no real choice. Not for the vast majority."

After his stinging indictment of the system that he'd worked in for twenty five years, Dave gulped down the last of his pint and said, "Anyway, my good friends, I'm off to the gents and will see you in the car park presently."

Once Dave had gone, Tom said, "I was going to ask -"

"Yes?" said Françoise.

"Are you going to be at the do, tonight?"

"Yes, I am."

"I was wondering ..."

"Yes?"

"Well, I was just wondering if you might, perhaps, like to meet for a drink first?"

Françoise smiled like the Maja and said, "That would be very pleasant; I'd like that."

Tom, smiled back, finished his beer and they made their way to the car park.

Later they did, indeed, meet for a drink, at the new wine bar in town and enjoyed getting to know each other even better. Then they moved on to the French Bistro for the staff do which was, as usual, a sedate affair at first, but soon degenerated into an embarrassment of Bacchanalian drunkenness, that even surpassed previous years, fuelled by the rumour spreading, that there definitely wouldn't be an inspection until the autumn term.

This was the only excuse they all needed to swill down innumerable gallons of wine, beer and spirits, only for several of them to throw it all back up again, most of whom managed to make it to the toilets first, except for poor Susan Shepherd, who didn't, and was sick all over a potted philodendron. After this, however she felt much better and excelled at the Karaoke, which she won, hands down, with her version of the Dusty Springfield classic, 'I only want to be with you,' which she sang to her partner, Angela, re-creating all of Dusty's idiosyncratic hand movements and finally bursting into tears and snogging Angela's face off. The performance and the snogging received rapturous applause from all the staff, who were amazed at the extent to which, her coming out as a lesbian, really had brought her out of herself. These last few weeks had been a rite of passage for Susan and Angela and they would both remember them for the rest of their lives.

So would Linda and Andy. Françoise had sworn at him whenever she had come close, most recently, when she and Tom had arrived at the Bistro that night. And Julia had rubbed his nose in the mess by openly flirting with Dick. But Andy's lonely trip to Coventry was only finally broken by Linda approaching him and calling a truce. They actually sat next to each other for the meal and, of course, spent much of the time studying a new scan photo of the embryo and speculating over the future of their child. Linda had been to the maternity clinic that very day, and was able to inform Andy that the baby was a boy. His ego had taken a severe beating in recent times but, hearing that he was going to be the father of a male child, made in his image, had a restorative effect like no other, and Andy began to, at least, consider the possibility of settling down, something that would have been utterly unthinkable a few weeks before. Linda, on the other hand, had been through the trauma of several unsuccessful attempts at IVF, with her ex-partner Charlie and now, finally falling pregnant, naturally (if having sex with Andy could come into that category) she'd quickly developed a sneaking admiration for him and, at the very least, the fortitude and fecundity of his sperm, even though he'd been a two timing bastard.

♦ ♦ ♦

The morning after, the clock in the empty staff room read 08.30 on July 14th. Dave was the first to arrive wearing dark glasses and feeling queasy. He looked at the clock and thought two thoughts: first, that everybody would be arriving as late as possible after the previous night's excess and secondly, that the French friends he spent his summer holidays with would be celebrating Bastille Day. It might be 'Le jour de gloire,' in Paris and the Dordogne but it was most definitely more like 'Le jour de vomissement' at Southgreen, with the number of hungover, sick people who were soon about to gather for the staff briefing. Dave was making himself a black coffee, when Sebastian joined him in the kitchen area and popped an Alka Selzer into a glass of water, waiting for it to fizz away before downing it in one, similar to the way he had gulped down several pints of ale the night before.

Andy then arrived and went to look at the notice board, before saying, "Françoise," almost pleading with her to acknowledge him, as she entered the room, also wearing shades. She didn't miss the opportunity to say, "Vous êtes merde" to Andy and then ignored him and went to make a drink. He decided to give the briefing a miss and left, nearly crashing into Tom who swerved saying, "Steady on!"

Helga arrived and ignored everyone, crossing to the Principal's office and closing the door behind her.

Bethany entered her office from the door to the corridor, as she didn't want to have to chat to Helga. She delved into her handbag to get a fizzy vitamin C tablet but thought better of it and unlocked the drawer of her desk. She removed the bottle of scotch and undid it, saying, "Hair of the dog," before taking a large swig and replacing it in the drawer. She sprayed her mouth and neck with perfume and then entered Helga's area and walked straight past her into the staff room, with her secretary following on, close behind.

Mr Bull entered the staff room from another door at the back of the computer stations. He was still very much the worse for wear and had already been sick while he had fed swill to the pigs at 6 am. They didn't mind however and Vanessa had politely and helpfully sorted it out, licking up the vomit with relish before returning to suckle Dinsdale and her other piglets. Mr Bull was about to heave again but made a U turn and headed straight back out.

As he left, Dick Fenwick came in, dishevelled, wearing the same, now creased and crumpled suit that he had worn the previous evening.

Finally, Evan Dylan, better known by his various nicknames, as Mr Tambourine Man, Swansea Jack and Bob the Builder, entered, looking very smart, in a brand new, crisp, dark suit, sporting a bright, Bugs Bunny tie saying, in his inimitable Welsh way, "Morning everybody. Lovely day for it, though heavy rain forecast for later. Hope you're all feeling better than you look. It's my interview for Mr Hill's job today so, it's lucky really, I had to stick to mineral water last night."

With this, every person in the room, as one, picked up the nearest object to hand and threw it at Mr Dylan. Paper cups from the water dispenser, magazines, fruit of various varieties, from grapes to seedless satsumas, even a packet of Mr Hill's beloved Cheeselets, which hit him full in the face. Moreover, Susan Shepherd, who had arrived late, looking decidedly pasty and not knowing what was really going on, threw a large lump of blu tack at him and then felt guilty and put her hand over her mouth in horror at what she had done. The result of this reaction was that Mr Dylan became convinced that, with the stiff competition he was about to face from two Oxbridge graduates, it just wasn't going to be his day.

Sebastian was finding the briefing that followed particularly difficult. "Just to remind you all," he said, "there's a full meeting of the School Council Forum at quarter to twelve today, in the main school hall. It's important that all council delegates and observers are reminded at registration, so if all group tutors, I mean mentors, I mean what does it really matter what they're called, you know what I bloody well mean, please, just remind them, will you."

Bethany, feeling just as fragile as her deputy said, "Thank you, Sebastian. Also, a special reminder that interviews are being held today, so please be polite to strangers, as they may be a candidate for the post of Head of Science. Any questions? Support staff? Susan? Or should we be calling you Dusty in future?" Susan blushed. "Next thing we know you'll be wearing eye shadow and back combing your hair." Susan giggled. "No questions? No, as usual have a nice day every –" but before she could get to the end of the word she stopped, looking with terrified eyes, towards the main door, where she saw Mr Harris and Dr Sonia Sims, framed in the entrance.

"Good morning, Ms Sedgeford; everybody," said Mr Harris. "Dr Sims and I would like to have a look around if that's alright. We decided this would be an excellent day for our inspection. No need for anyone to worry. We just want to see a normal day at Southgreen Academy. Three other members of our inspection team are just signing in at Reception"

"Of course if we'd have had some warning, we'd have organised a proper welcoming party," said Sebastian, in his most ingratiating, Basil like manner yet, underneath, he was furious. "Would you like a cup of coffee first or –?"

"No, thank you," replied Dr Sims "We'll see your Mentoring Registration Groups and then we'd like to start where we last left off, if we may, and have a look at your new Drama Studio."

"Mr Carter's your man for that," said Sebastian. "Did I tell you, he's a professional actor?"

"Yes, you did," replied Mr Harris.

"Just got a part in the 'stranger danger' campaign," said Sebastian, jollily, though he was steering into stormy waters. "Funny, when you think about it, he's the nasty monster kids shouldn't accept sweets from, lurking outside the school gates, and he's actually teaching at Southgreen! Sure some of the parents will get confused by that, but it's the price you have to pay for quality. Let me introduce you to Mr Carter, if I may."

And after Mentoring Registration, that's exactly what Sebastian did.

♦ ♦ ♦

Three chairs were set up opposite the Principal's office and three, very stiff bodies were perched on them. Evan Dylan was sandwiched, in between Duncan Lancaster and Simon Warwick, who were not only Oxbridge graduates, but also very upper class Oxbridge graduates. Mr Dylan might have been considered a monumental bore by the vast majority of the staff at Southgreen but, you had to hand it to him, he was doing his best to engage them in polite conversation. But whatever he said, he got the same response from his rival candidates. It was either a "Yes," which sounded to Mr Dylan like "Ee-ess," or "No," which sounded like "Knee-oh."

It took them an age to say anything at all until Mr Dylan finally broke the ice by saying, "It's the waiting that's always the worst part isn't it?"

There was no response for several seconds until Mr Lancaster and Mr Warwick both said, "Ee-ess."

Having managed a brief conversation with them earlier in the car park, Mr Dylan then said, it felt like an age later, "Yes, Chipping Sodbury is a long drive from here. Very long. A lot further than

Reigate" Again there was a long pause before Mr Warwick said, "Ee-ess."

It was an uphill struggle for the Welshman and his rivals' snootiness was beginning to undermine his confidence, knowing how highly qualified they both were. But give him credit, Mr Evan Dylan was wearing his heart upon his sleeve and said, "I know I've been here years but she's only just arrived see. I'm not giving you too much help by saying that she values loyalty beyond all else. Anyway the best of luck or break a leg as they say to performers and, let's face it, what are we if we're not performers?"

Quickly and together, Mr Lancaster and Mr Warwick both said, "Ee-ess!"

Encouraged by their approbation Mr Dylan kept going saying, "Whatever you do, don't dry up."

"Knee-oh," said Mr Lancaster.

"Just keep going."

"Ee-ess," said Mr Warwick.

"It's when you stiffen up that you get problems, I always find."

"Ee-ess," said the two, already extremely stiff candidates. They seemed to have first class degrees in rigidity.

"I decided to wear my lucky Bugs Bunny tie. I wore it the day I got the job of second in the department, see. Not that I'm superstitious or anything."

"Knee-oh," said Mr Warwick.

"Knee-oh," repeated Mr Lancaster.

Mr Dylan was going to continue but was stopped by Helga entering the staff room, smiling, saying, "Mr Dylan, Ms Sedgeford and the panel will see you first. Alphabetical order. Then Mr Lancaster and finally, you, Mr Warwick."

"Thenx," said Mr Warwick, which was, at least, different.

"Thenx," said Mr Lancaster, which wasn't.

Evan entered the cauldron with Helga, leaving the two Oxbridge candidates to stew, but after a short time Brian Bull came into the staff room and saw them sat bolt upright in their chairs.

"Don't suppose either of you have seen Mr Swinton, the Vice Principal, have you?" There was a lengthy pause before Mr Lancaster said, "Knee-oh," followed almost immediately by Mr Warwick saying, "Knee-oh."

"It's just that there's terrible weather forecast," said Mr Bull. "Torrential rain later with possible flooding. It'll be wet weather play and lunchtime with kids trampling mud everywhere, more than likely. Just what we need on the day of inspection in the middle of July. Anyway, if you see him perhaps you could pass it on."

"Ee-ess," said Mr Lancaster.

"Good luck with the interviews," said Mr Bull, though he thought to himself that this pair wouldn't exactly fit in at Southgreen.

"Thenx," said Mr Lancaster.

"Thenx," said Mr Warwick.

♦ ♦ ♦

At mid-morning break, Bethany was hearing about their first lesson observation from Mr Harris, Dr Sims and Sebastian.

"I told you he wouldn't disappoint you," said Sebastian. "Quality, is our young Mr Carter. Had my doubts about him at first but he's overcome his teething problems and he's delivering the goods in no uncertain manner."

"Yes," said Dr Sims, "I was very impressed with how he got them to evaluate their improvisations."

Mr Harris agreed and then said "That boy, Peter Sutcliffe, really was able to convey the awful dilemma of such a tragic story, in a most mature way."

"Ms Sedgeford, you should have seen it," said Dr Sims "He was so moving when finally, he couldn't bring himself to kill the two children, even though he despised their scientist father for the research he was doing on monkeys."

"Yes," said Mr Harris. "And that boy, Ricky Knapp, was excellent as the monkey being lobotomised. His whimpering was filled with such extraordinary pathos."

"Did you think so?" said Sebastian. "I thought he sounded more like a dog but then I'm no Richard Attenborough. Miriam Stiff was also very arresting, I thought, when she pleaded for her daughter's life and said that she was against the cruelty too, but it was her husband's job, so what could she do? And how were we ever going to cure all the terrible diseases in the world?"

"And when that boy, Carl, finally blew the scientist's head off with a twelve bore," said Dr Sims, "there was real menace in his eyes."

"Yes, Ms Sedgeford," said Mr Harris, "it really was very impressive indeed."

"Our only criticism would be a lack of evidence of planning," said Dr Sims "Mr Carter said that Mr Swinton had told him that he'd had instructions from the highest authority to 'throw those silly plans away.' "

Sebastian gave Bethany a look fit to kill and then said, "Nonsense, I said nothing of the kind and anyway, you do realise that Mr Carter is a supply teacher, who has stepped in at the last minute?"

"Of course, how silly of me," said Dr Sims "Well, the same rules don't quite apply then. How are the interviews going Ms Sedgeford?"

"Just got to observe Mr Warwick's teaching and then we'll be done," said Bethany. "It's the School Council Forum at quarter to twelve. I do hope you'll come. Peter Sutcliffe is proposing a motion to close the school farm; not a chance of succeeding, of course, but you should see some fireworks. It's all good debating fun. Democracy in action."

"We look forward to it," said Mr Harris.

♦ ♦ ♦

Peter Sutcliffe had had several long chats with Dave Hardman in the previous weeks. He was impressed with his teacher's veganism and thought that he would try to befriend him, so much so, that he insisted on testing the Head of English and the Performing Arts by repeatedly calling him by his first name. Dave was not one to be put off by this and didn't mind the informality, which drew Peter even closer. They talked about music and Peter explained the workings of his new iPod to him. Dave found it amazing to think that Peter could hold a thousand songs in the palm of his hand. They talked about the music that they liked and Peter was fascinated by the psychedelic sounds of the nineteen sixties. He had downloaded the Jefferson Airplane song based on 'Alice in Wonderland,' as Dave had suggested, and loved the power of Grace Slick's voice. Also, instantly, he had become a big fan of "The Incredible String Band," again on Dave's recommendation, and downloaded several of their songs with tokens he'd been given for his birthday. To cement their new found friendship, in Peter's eyes, Dave had also sold him a second ticket to see ' 'Tis Pity She's a Whore,' at the National Theatre, as there weren't many other students interested. Peter said he was going to invite his girlfriend, but when Dave pressed him about the identity of the person he clammed up. Similarly, when Dave asked him how the pyrotechnics for the summer fair were coming along, all Peter would say was that it was a surprise.

Now, during period three on Bastille Day, Peter was thinking about his ambitious plans, sat behind his easel in the 'A' Level Art studio. It had started to rain heavily and the sound of large raindrops falling was amplified by them hitting the windows and corrugated tin roof of this Southgreen outbuilding. It was fitting therefore that the lyrics he was hearing through his earphones, were from The Incredible String Band song about a box of paints, which alluded to the artist telling the drops of rain falling on the windows that this was no time for tears. So, as Françoise Poitin sat, resplendent in her clothed Maja pose, on the chaise longue, again Peter was oblivious to what she was saying.

"I was honoured to find your invitation, Peter, in my pigeon hole, but I'm afraid I must respectfully decline," said Françoise. She waited for what seemed like an eternity for Peter to reply, but had become used to the taciturn manner in which Peter conducted these portrait sessions and so continued as if he had actually asked why?

"It just wouldn't be right, Peter, for me to go alone with you to London to see ' 'Tis Pity She's a Whore,' because you are only fifteen and I am a teacher and, anyway, those tickets are for school students and not for people like me."

Françoise waited for a response, in fear that Peter would be upset, but it didn't materialise. The sound of the rain intensified and grew considerably louder, which brought goose pimples out on her skin and made her shiver momentarily, so that she moved and re-arranged the gold and black blouse that was draped around her shoulders.

"Anyway, what if I have a boyfriend, Peter," she continued, "what would I say to him? 'Sorry, I'm going to see ' 'Tis Pity She's a Whore' with this handsome chap, Peter Sutcliffe'." She took a second before saying, "And it's not Mr Bailey; I can tell that's what you're thinking."

There was a long pause before another faint rumbling of thunder. Peter continued to wield his brush with confidence, unaware that his invitation had been turned down.

"Can you hear thunder?" asked Françoise.

The sound reverberated. "Yes, there it is again," she confirmed, looking towards the window and seeing the amazing contrast, where the previously golden, shining sun and bright blue sky had suddenly converged with the livid, dark blue, grey and black cumulonimbus clouds. It was spectacular!

"Peter you should look out of the window," said Françoise. "If you had chosen to reconstruct one of William Turner's landscape paintings, you'd have the perfect scene to paint right now. The colours are so vivid, Peter and the light almost biblical." If she was hoping for some sort of agreement she would be disappointed, as Peter continued in his silent, diffident way, not making a sound, except for cursing when he made a mistake or mixing the paint with his knife on the palette, to get the required colour.

Suddenly, there was a bright, intense flash of forked lightning. The main lights in the art studio, as well as the lights dimly illuminating the painting's subject, flickered on and off but finally returned, just as a great clap of thunder shook the building's foundations

Unbeknown to Françoise, the whole experience of posing for Peter was becoming something of a major catharsis and all the frustrations and anger of the last few weeks were coming to the surface, brought on by the unyielding power of the storm.

"Thunder can make you mad, they say," said Françoise, her mind racing and recalling Andy's nasty antics involving Peter. She remained silent for some seconds before saying, "I hate Mr Bailey for making you run round the field twelve times and causing you to get so breathless." She paused again. "It was so cruel of him to take your asthma inhaler, Peter, and you were most gallant to refuse to apologise." She was beginning to seethe inwardly, thinking about the sex that she and Andy had had together. Her stomach was now churning.

She continued to berate him, saying, "The nude is the most famous art form, so who is Mr Randy Andy Bailey to tell you, me or anyone else what we should do with our bodies?"

There was another irradiating flash of lightning followed, only a few seconds later by an enormous explosion of thunder; the loudest so far.

"When I was a child I used to like it when there was a torrential storm and the thunder cracked like this," she said, as her mind took her back to her youth in rural France. "We lived in a very isolated place, Peter, in the heart of the countryside and sometimes, in a storm, I would take off all my clothes and run outside into the rain. I would stand there jumping, naked in the puddles, laughing and drinking the raindrops, and my mother would shout for me to come in and tell me off!" She stopped and the expression of reverie on the Maja's face changed as if she was now experiencing her own epiphany. "Do you know, Peter," she said with joy, "I have just had a brilliant idea!"

She got up from the chaise longue and faced the easel which still obscured Peter from her sight. "Paint me naked, Peter," she said. "Just like Goya. The clothed Maja and the nude Maja. A contrast. That's what I want, Peter. Paint me like this!" And with those words or, more precisely, the actions that followed them, Peter was hurled into a state of utter distraction and confusion, for Françoise Poitin quickly and deftly removed her golden blouse and white dress and stood there, naked, wearing only her flesh coloured knickers from Marks and Spencer. She then got back onto the chaise longue recreating her previous pose but was suddenly taken by surprise, as the easel crashed to the floor and Peter rushed off out of the studio.

Getting up, Françoise shouted after him, "Peter. Peter!" But he was gone.

Simultaneously, from behind the screen that stood opposite, Tom Carter entered saying, "Françoise, I was going to ask if you were free this –"

"Tom," said Françoise, quickly covering herself with her dress and picking up all of her clothes.

"You did it then?" said Tom, smiling. "Not such a spoilsport!"

"It would appear not," replied Françoise, smiling back.

They heard voices. It was Mr Harris and Dr Sims. Françoise, panicking, frantically began to dress. Tom nipped behind the screen.

"We're looking for Mr Latham. We seem to be a bit lost," said Mr Harris. Arriving through the door he continued, "I wonder if you could. Oh I didn't mean to–"

Francoise was half in, half out of her dress, and pulled it up to cover her breasts.

"I'm just changing, Mr Harris!"

Oh, I'm terribly sorry," said the Chief Inspector.

Tom emerged from behind the screen. "Mademoiselle Poitin has been posing as a life model for Peter Sutcliffe's reconstruction of Goya's clothed Maja masterpiece," he said, saving the day.

"So we can see," said Dr Sims, acerbically.

Tom crossed to the easel and picked it up. Then he rescued Peter's painting and held it aloft, showing the clothed Maja to both Françoise and the inspectors. Mr Harris and Dr Sims studied the painting and then looked across to Françoise. In unison they both said, "Very impressive."

Dr Sims added, "Very impressive indeed." Then she and Mr Harris headed for the exit.

As the inspectors left, Tom and Françoise smiled at each other. After they had gone, Tom looked directly into the eyes of the, now fully clothed, Maja and kissed her on her cherry, red lips.

♦ ♦ ♦

Peter Sutcliffe couldn't believe what he had just seen. He was in turmoil and had no time to gather his thoughts and to put into perspective what had just happened. After all, he had originally asked Mademoiselle Poitin to pose nude for him, even though he had no expectation of his request being accepted. He was thinking about whether she would now accompany him to see ' 'Tis Pity She's a Whore,' not having heard her say that she couldn't possibly do such a thing, as he'd had the sounds of The Incredible String Band ringing in his ears. But his mind had no time to dwell on these events, as now he had to focus entirely on the School Council Forum and his motion to close the school farm. Not only that, but he had other plans afoot.

Mr Harris and Dr Sonia Sims were also a little confused, to say the least, by what they had encountered so far at Southgreen Academy. It was turning out to be a far more unconventional institution than they had anticipated. They were both taken aback and rather unsettled by the seemingly progressive interpretation of rules and conventions but, at the same time, they were witnessing some examples of exemplary practice. It was lunchtime now and the school was hampered by the torrential rain which meant all the students were confined inside. Having said that there was much toing and froing from one building to another and that meant that the children did indeed trample mud everywhere, as Mr Bull had told Mr Lancaster and Mr Warwick.

The canteen was a picture of raucous behaviour, worthy of a Bruegel painting but two students helpfully guided the inspectors on a safe journey through the mayhem. They even managed to buy some food and were both impressed by the quality of the lunch menu and complimented the dinner ladies. They sat amid the bedlam and, while eating, talked to students about the amazing School Council Forum that they had been present at, after their visit to the art department.

This was the subject of conversation too in Bethany's office, where the Principal was telling Sebastian all about it.

"It was pandemonium, Sebastian. Peter Sutcliffe had whipped them up into a frenzied mob with his Power Point presentation of terrible images of animal cruelty. They were chanting, 'Close the farm, close the farm,' and when it came to the vote, some of them must have been intimidated because it was a tie! I had to use my casting vote as chairperson to reject the proposal."

"I bet he loved that."

"Exactly," said Bethany. "He started shouting 'fix' and 'whitewash.' Then, rather curiously, he said something you're always saying, Seb."

"Really?"

"Yes, really. He said, 'stupidity always has its repercussions. You have been warned' and stormed out of the hall, followed by all the delegates opposed to the farm."

Just then, there was a knock at the door. "Come in," said Bethany.

Mr Harris and Dr Sims did so and Mr Harris entered saying, "Fireworks indeed, Ms Sedgeford!"

"Yes, I'm sorry about that," said Bethany.

"Don't apologise. The standard of debate was extremely high and most commendable and, even though it got rather heated, we thought you chaired the meeting in an exemplary fashion."

"Thank you," said Bethany, rather relieved.

"We were a bit taken aback however by what we witnessed before the Forum."

"And what was that, Mr Harris?" asked Bethany.

"Well, we appreciate that latterly it's all been in the cause of serious artistic endeavour, Ms Sedgeford, but every time we encounter Mademoiselle Poitin she is either in the company of others in a state of undress or, how can I put it ... she's in the buff herself!"

Bethany looked at Sebastian, whose face displayed the same level of shock and alarm that she was experiencing, but there was no need to enquire further, as they were literally saved by a bell that rang loudly and continuously.

"That's all we need," said Sebastian. "Someone's set off the fire alarm!"

◆ ◆ ◆

The entire school was lined up in the playground, in the teeming rain, in their Mentoring Registration Groups. Soaking wet teachers were running round with registers in hand and Helga was looking out for the raised arms of the same teachers, which signified that all were present and correct in their mentor group, in strict military fashion. She would then collect the registers and was able to assess who was and who wasn't present. She would then pass the information on to Sebastian. None of the children were supposed to talk, but rumours were rife and speculation about who had set the alarm off was buzzing around the congregation of extremely wet and miserable students. They weren't even missing lessons, which would have been some compensation, as it was still their lunch hour, and Sebastian Swinton was in no mood, on this, the day of a surprise inspection, to be at all lenient with any of them, even though the overwhelming majority hadn't done anything wrong. Anyway, he had come prepared with his raincoat on and was standing in front of the school, gathered before him, underneath a large golfing umbrella, holding a megaphone. He had also made sure that his Principal and the two inspectors, were furnished with the same protection from the inclement elements, and the thought had crossed his mind that Dr Sims and Mr Harris were certainly seeing the school warts and all, which, he was trying to persuade himself, was a good thing.

He looked down on the dripping faces of the children, staring them in the eye individually. He remained silent. This was what he called his 'Hitler' routine, which he prided himself on and had off to a T. After nearly a minute he started speaking, amplified by the megaphone.

"Yes, I know you don't like standing in the playground in the pouring rain, but stupidity has its repercussions! I don't like getting wet. You don't like getting wet. Ms Sedgeford doesn't like getting wet. None of the teachers, nor the support staff, nor the very important guests we have visiting us today like getting wet! But wet we will get and wet will we stay, until the person, or persons, who set the fire alarm off, does the decent thing and owns up."

No one said anything but the tension intensified as Helga passed a note to Sebastian, who read it and then leant across and whispered something in Bethany's ear.

"Right. Progress at last," he said. "It appears that Peter Sutcliffe, Carl Borman, Miriam Stiff and Maxine Dalton have chosen to absent themselves from our cosy little lunchtime gathering. They will not get away with this." Sebastian then honed in on one boy and stared at him saying, "Ricky Knapp, I'm surprised you're not with them but I'm sure that you know something about it, and may well have put them up to this, so get outside my office now!"

Ricky was rigid with fear and didn't move.

"Now boy, not tomorrow or next week!"

Ricky couldn't help himself and was just about to give his Hermann the dog impression, to elicit a modicum of sympathy, when Sebastian stopped him with, "And don't you start your whimpering!"

A wet and soggy, Ricky Knapp, crept off, as Sebastian continued.

"Right, without talking, I want you to lead off back to school in an organised and orderly fashion and congregate, in your mentor groups, ready for afternoon mentoring registration! Anyone who can't move away silently can join Ricky Knapp outside my office and spend a couple of hours after school under my supervision. In single file. You are dismissed!" With that, the perfectly straight lines of sodden, Mentoring Registration Groups moved off back into the main school building.

Mr Harris and Dr Sims were very impressed by both Sebastian Swinton's undoubted authority and the martial manner in which the students were dispersing. Their attention was distracted however by the sight of Mr Dylan approaching the Principal and her Vice Principal, in a state of some agitation.

"Here, have you seen these?" asked Mr Dylan, holding up a bunch of leaflets and passing a couple to Bethany and Sebastian. "They're all over the school. 'Stupidity always has its repercussions. It's stupid to have a farm. Close it now!!! You have been warned by the Southgreen Animal Liberation Army for Moral Integrity.' "

"SALAMI indeed," said Sebastian, now incandescent with rage. "Wish I could get my hands on a great, big Danish one and shove it right up Peter Sutcliffe's –"

But Mr Harris and Dr Sims were spared the last word of his sentence by Bethany snarling, "Sebastian!" They all started to move off back to the main building, just as Brian Bull came running across the playground, splattered with mud, looking alarmed.

"Whatever's the matter, Mr Bull?" asked Bethany.

"It's terrible, Ms Sedgeford, I don't know where to begin."

"What's terrible?" asked Bethany, scarcely believing that anything else could go wrong on this day of all days." But Brian Bull could hardly believe it either and was, temporarily, lost for words.

"Well?" said Bethany.

"Someone's let all the animals out!" said Mr Bull.

"What?"

"They've escaped!"

"I'll kill him!" said Sebastian.

"The fences are down in every field and all the sheep and cows have got out. Then while I'm chasing after them, stampeding now, I nearly get run over by Carl Borman, who's stolen my Land Rover and is towing a trailer load of pigs and chickens towards the main road. Anne Widdecombe and her piglets were staring out of the back looking like lambs to the slaughter. I tried to stop them but they splattered me with mud as they roared past."

"They?" asked Sebastian.

"Peter Sutcliffe, Miriam Stiff and Maxine Dalton all giving it large with the two fingers and the clenched fists." At that moment the strains of 'Old MacDonald had a farm,' could be heard from Mr Bull's ringtone. He answered. "Hello ... yes it is. Where? You're kidding ... No, I'll be right down there, Mr Sutton, thank you."

"Well?" asked Sebastian.

"It's Casanova," said Mr Bull. "He's got into a field of Mr Sutton's ewes and is having a right old time. I better get down there before he tups the lot of them!"

Bethany responded to Mr Bull's Elizabethan turn of phrase by saying, "We'll hold the fort here and arrange search parties to go out."

"Yes," said Sebastian. "We'll make the staff room the HQ."

"I'll get straight back to you," said Mr Bull.

"Don't you worry, Brian, we'll save our precious animals! This means all-out war," said Bethany as they arrived at the main entrance.

Sebastian was right in thinking that Ricky Knapp had more information about the events that were transpiring, but it had been a mistake for him to allow the boy to walk, unaccompanied, to wait outside his office. Ricky had taken a detour and gone into the school hall, before he had followed the Vice Principal's orders. There he had slipped the CD, which Peter Sutcliffe had given him for this very purpose, into the hall's sound system and had pressed the repeat button and turned up the volume to maximum, before rushing off to comply with Sebastian's instruction. He nearly bumped into the Vice Principal but managed to avoid him and the inspectors, as they entered the school to the sound of 'La Marseillaise,' blaring from the PA system. 'Allons enfants de la Patrie, Le jour de gloire est arrivé.' And arrived, it certainly had!

The first discernible sign of this was when Sebastian entered the empty staff room, alone, only to be confronted by two chickens, pecking at some Cheeselets that Mr Hill had dropped earlier, as he was being stirred from his slumber by a distraught Susan Shepherd. This was a notable first, as nobody had ever managed to wake Mr Hill when he was suffering from the symptoms of narcolepsy. But the vision of Mr Hill dying from smoke inhalation or worse, sitting in his chair, was both too much for Susan to contemplate and enough for her to whisper two words in his ear and then shake him with such force that he woke up and started to lash out at her, shouting, "Where, where?" before she could avail him of the urgency of the situation. Some of the Cheeselets had also fallen onto his reclining chair and one of the chickens jumped up and pecked at them furiously. Just as Sebastian was coming to terms with this image, a beautiful, grey Angora rabbit could be seen hopping down from the computer stations and leaving small, spherical rabbit turds on the carpet. Just then, the staff room phone rang. Sebastian was going to give short shrift to anyone.

"No, I'm afraid they're all out chasing animals at the moment, goodbye" he said, and was just about to replace the receiver, when he realised his mistake and continued, saying, "Sorry, did you say Superintendent? ... well, there's no need to shout ... you must be, yes, Superintendent Lockhart ...yes ... we've got every available member of staff out looking ... yes, we think we do know how it happened ... yes ...outside ASDA? ... Look, I'd better get Mr Bull, our farm manager, onto it straightaway."

As if by instruction from Basil, Mr Bull and Dick Fenwick appeared and took a fowl each. Mr Bull knew just how to catch the chickens and, as it happened, actually knew these two by name. They were Florence and Felicity. He caught both of them, one in each arm and then passed one to Dick who, by accepting the gift, had widened his life experience significantly. Françoise, arrived and managed to rescue the rabbit.

"Mr Bull's just dealing with some animals in the staff room as we speak," said Sebastian. "Two arrests? ... No! Really, the things people will do."

Superintendent Lockhart wanted more information.

"Yes, I can give you their names but can we keep this confidential? We don't want this getting out all over the ... already has? ...television news? ... no, I haven't ... yes, I know that taking and driving away is an arrestable offence ... yes, alright then ... Peter Sutcliffe ... yes, as in the Yorkshire Ripper, yes ... spelt the same, yes, extraordinary ... parents ... I know, yes, why don't they stop to think ...yes ... it's Carl Borman ... wearing a beret and a Che Guevara bandana ... he's the driver ... Yes, Miriam Stiff and Maxine Dalton ... no, that's D for Dalton. Yes, that's right, Superintendent."

Mr Bull returned to the staff room and Sebastian pointed to the phone and said to the Superintendent, "Speak to Mr Bull now would you, Superintendent Lockhart," passing the phone to Mr Bull, as Bethany, Helga, Mr Dylan and the inspectors all appeared.

"Yes, superintendent?" said Mr Bull. There was a lengthy pause while he took in what was being said; horrified. "Outside? ... I will, I'll be down as soon as possible. It's chaos here. I've given your lot our mobile numbers. Yes. Keep you posted. Bye." Mr Bull turned to the others and said, "There are sheep grazing on the roundabout outside ASDA!"

"No," said Bethany.

"Well," said Helga, "at least they're not inside ASDA," adding, "they'd probably get better service than I do."

Sebastian expanded on his phone call, filling Bethany in on the detail. "Just the two arrests so far, boss. Our friendly, local market butcher, Mr Bass, has been caught, red handed, pushing one of our prize beef cattle onto the back of his wagon."

"I'm never going to him again," said Helga to Mr Harris. "You can never trust what you get in the market, these days, can you?"

"And, this will make you laugh," said Sebastian, trying to extract a terrible, black humour from the situation, "A trail of cockerel feathers along the High Street, led a constable to the back of the local fried chicken shop, where he caught the owner, bang to rights, wielding a bloodstained machete."

"They were free range, them! Too good for fried chicken takeaways," said Mr Bull, worried how many more fatalities there might be.

"Well," said Sebastian, the sound of 'La Marseillaise' ringing in his ears, "on this historic day, what better way for the English to celebrate the storming of the Bastille, than by beheading cockerels, the symbol of the French! Eh, Mademoiselle Poitin?"

Françoise thought this was very insensitive and so, by his look, did Mr Bull, so she said, "I thought we were trying to save the animals, Mr Swinton!"

"Any news on the pigs?" Bethany enquired.

"Not yet," said Mr Bull. "It's Anne Widdecombe and Vanessa Feltz that I'm worried about. Jo Brand is very adaptable and Lisa Riley and Hattie Jacques are both level headed but Annie and Vanessa can be very temperamental."

"Well come on," said Bethany. "We've all got work to do." Sebastian then delegated Dave and Tom, who had just returned from registering their students, to go with Françoise and Mr Dylan and he then accompanied a group comprising Bethany, the inspectors, Mr Bull, Andy Bailey and Dick Fenwick.

Amazingly, Mr Hill was still wide awake, having been roused from his narcolepsy by Susan Shepherd, who obviously had the golden touch in re-charging his batteries, which had been seriously depleted, after a long morning on the interview panel. They were both asked to look after a large group of Year 9 pupils in the gymnasium.

◆ ◆ ◆

Because of the wet weather, Dave's Honda Accord wouldn't start when his group got to the car park, so they all piled into Françoise's Citroen 2 CV, with the stripy red, white and blue roof, the colours of the French tricolour. This was apt, it being Bastille Day and with them going in search of Peter and his band of sans-culottes, known by the whole school now as SALAMI! Mr Dylan was sitting in the back with Tom, busily putting Mr Bull's mobile number on speed dial, as well as the number for Sheila, one of the lab technicians in the science department, so he could keep the channels of communication open. The rain was torrential still and the thunder rumbled continuously, interspersed with great flashes of lightning, which looked as if they would strike the car at any moment. Françoise put an Elton John compilation into the old cassette player, trying to normalise their situation and dispelling the worry of them all being struck by a billion volt electric shock.

There was a long traffic jam in the direction of the town so Dave, who knew his way around the rat runs said, "Turn right here," and Françoise, pulled hard on the steering wheel, only just avoiding an oncoming van, and turned down a narrow street, that veered off into a lane, that headed out into the countryside.

"They'll make for Chapel Bank, I'll bet," said Dave. "They'll go by Bidhurst Woods." The 2CV was at top speed and Françoise had a job to see, even with the lights on, it being so dark and wet, but she was still slow and two police cars overtook her at speed, their sirens sounding and blue lights flashing.

"Looks as if we're going the right way then," said Dave. "Just keep those lights in your sights, Françoise and follow them." She stepped hard on the accelerator teasing out all the speed that the 2CV could muster, as Elton John sang a song about a journey to meet a pilot while a helicopter circled overhead. Passing close by Bidhurst Woods Tom said, "Look, one of the police cars has pulled over there."

Dave turned back to look but said, "Keep going, Françoise. I'm pretty certain they'll be heading for Chapel Bank." Sure enough, as they skidded round a hairpin bend they could see the other police car racing ahead.

It was uphill now but the lane was flooded and Françoise was having to deal with a river of water coming towards them down the hill, steering the car into the middle of the road to avoid it. She looked into her mirror and saw the flashing light of a police Range Rover. Sounding its siren and hooting its horn for her to get out of the way, it overtook her and turned sharp left down a farm track.

"They're taking the pretty route," said Dave. "It's a long way round, that way, but only a four wheel drive will be able to negotiate the way up Chapel Bank."

As they continued on up the hill, following the other police car, Tom looked out of the rear window and said, "There's what appears to be a white minibus catching us up."

"That'll probably be Basil and the others," replied Dave, just as they were reaching the brow of the hill.

The police car had pulled into a picnic area and viewpoint known locally as, Pillory Mound. "Stop here," said Dave. Françoise, pulled in to see two policemen, on foot, racing across the fields in front of them, their car parked near to a stile by a large wooden gate.

Just then, Mr Tambourine Man's mobile phone rang. The others jumped out of the 2CV, leaving the engine running, with speakers blaring and followed after the policemen. Mr Dylan, was given some very distressing news by Sheila, the Lab technician, and by the time he'd finished his conversation, Françoise, Dave and Tom had disappeared over a field beyond and behind a cluster of trees. Nevertheless, encouraged by Elton John's voice, now urging a rabbit named Jack to get a move on he climbed over the stile and started running, but in totally the wrong direction, heading away from the others! Swansea Jack might have been in the running for the Head of Science job but he would never make Head of Geography!

Beyond the trees, Dave said, "Seen anything?"

"No," replied Tom as they paused for breath, the rain still pouring down, accompanied by flashes of lightning that were now very close by indeed, as the time between the forks illuminating the sky and the rumbling thunder was getting less with every sequence.

As they were heading further uphill, they all knew they were in danger, which prompted Françoise to say, "We must find Peter and the others before something terrible happens. Come on." And with that they continued on their chase of the 'sans-culottes.'

The minibus arrived and parked by the other two cars, as Mr Bull's Old MacDonald ringtone rang out once more. "Hello ... Mr Doyle ... yes, we've stopped by Pillory Mound. Weather's atrocious still ... have you checked Boris? No, he never has! Have a good look would you? ... Well that's better news anyway. I'll get back to you." Ending the call he said, "That's all the sheep accounted for but Boris has gone missing!"

"Not dear little Boris," said a distraught Bethany, as Old MacDonald sounded off again.

"Hello, Bob," said Mr Bull. "Have they? I'm sorry about that but it's a relief. At least I know where they are. How many? Yes, twenty two, that's right ... could you? I really appreciate it. Bye for now."

Brian turned to Bethany and the others and said, "The Jersey dairy herd have all been found; they'd got onto Bob Edwards' land and he's bringing them back.

His phone rang again. "Hello, yes, Superintendent Lockhart ... yes, I've been talking to him ... yes, well Mr Doyle could probably come, he's very experienced with the cattle, I'm up at Pillory Mound, where your lot are ... No, that's terrible ... we don't want them getting in there ... we have to stop them, Superintendent. I'll head on down there, now."

As the call finished Bethany said, "What's wrong, Brian?"

"There's gridlock in the High Street. The Herefords are holding up the traffic and won't move. I'll have to get Mr Doyle down there pronto but there's even worse Ms Sedgeford."

Bethany couldn't conceive of anything being worse than that but asked, "What?"

"Peter and his motley crew, driving the Land Rover and a trailer full of pigs, have been chased by two police cars heading towards Bidhurst Woods. They've disconnected the trailer and released the pigs and are now driving over rough terrain up to Chapel Bank. The police helicopter's keeping them in its sights, as the cars can't make it up there but the lightning's not helping."

Sebastian was standing just outside the minibus, leaning on a gate, looking through a pair of large binoculars. "I can see a police Range Rover now, at the bottom of the bank, but it's a fair distance away still. Some trees are obscuring my view," he said.

"We have to go," said Mr Bull. "There's wild boar down there! If Vanessa gets wind there's a bit of rough down in Bidhurst Woods, then we'll probably never see her again! Or any of the others, more than likely. I have to get back down there, right now. Who's coming with me? I'm going to need help."

For Mr Harris and Dr Sims, the choice of either trying to capture escaping pigs, in dense woodland where there were wild boar roaming, or alternatively, viewing the spectacle of apparently delinquent, Southgreen teenagers being chased by teachers and the local police force, was not one they had thought they'd be making at 3 o'clock on the afternoon of their inspection. It being the middle of July, they had come appropriately dressed for hot weather but they decided to stay put and so, got out of the minibus with Bethany, clutching their golfing umbrellas. Dick Fenwick and Andy Bailey, volunteered to help find the pigs and before you could say, 'apple sauce,' Mr Bull had reversed the vehicle and, with wheels spinning in the mud, headed off back down towards Bidhurst Woods.

The sky was still the colour of dark blue ink, highlighted with grey, but the rumbling thunder and flashes of lightning seemed more distant now. A police helicopter was hovering overhead but, every now and then it would turn away, after another flash lit up the livid sky. A flock of geese flew low, silhouetted in the magic light show, circling like harbingers of doom.

"At least the rain's easing off," said Dave, standing on a stile leading to another field over to Chapel Bank. "That's them!" he said.

"Where?" said Tom

"They've dumped the Land Rover and they're racing up Chapel Bank. They're all struggling with something."

"Looks like a big box," said Françoise. "Let's cut across this field." And they ran off.

A couple of fields away, Mr Dylan was lost and completely miserable. He had hoped to be celebrating his new found status of Head of Science by this time of the day or, alternatively, to have been licking the wounds of rejection, but no news was definitely not good news. He turned to look through three hundred and sixty degrees but couldn't see anyone, as the visibility was terrible. There was nothing else for it, so he shouted, "Hello!" There was no response. He climbed onto a pile of logs and balanced, precariously, shouting again, "Hello." Still no response. Then he did the same again but this time got a white hanky from his pocket and waved it above his head, as he screamed, "Hello. I'm lost. Hello, can you hear me?"

Sebastian was looking through his binoculars and caught a glimpse of the moving arc of the hanky, but it was the unmistakable lilt of Swansea Jack's Welsh accent that caused him to shout back, "Over here, Mr Dylan, over here!" He took another look through his large field glasses, which were impressive and worthy of having belonged to Field Marshall Montgomery himself. Had he been able to pick out the detail on Mr Dylan's face he would have seen a broad smile of relief, but instead he saw the intrepid Welshman a second later tripping over a log, stubbing his big toe and falling, flat on his face, into a large circular, and now recently moistened, cow pat. Sebastian hardly bothered to stifle his laughter before he saw Mr Dylan clambering up, running back towards them, his brand new interview suit now covered in mud, with Bugs Bunny looking dirty, smelly and decidedly pissed off! And, if the comic rabbit had asked, what was up, Mr Dylan would have replied, 'Everything!' Little did he know that events were going to take a turn for the worse before they got any better!

Bethany, who had her own smaller pair of binoculars, had witnessed this and was perched on the large gate next to the stile, surveying the scene.

Sebastian swivelled round a few degrees and said, "There they are! Sutcliffe and his SALAMI mob! They're struggling with something. Can't see what it is. Sutcliffe's pointing overhead to a flock of wild geese, flying up towards the top of the bank. They're following them." Little did Sebastian know that the geese were confirming Peter's, Bob Dylan inspired, premonition nor that they were the gaggle of geese from the school farm, that had been frightened into flight by a herd of stampeding Herefords.

"Miriam Stiff and Maxine, what's her name, are helping lift whatever it is, now," said Bethany, at which point Sebastian's phone rang.

"Yes, Superintendent Lockhart, it is … no, I didn't know that, no … thanks for letting me … yes, well we'll just have to add it to the list of criminal acts that these four hoodlums seem to wish to be taken into consideration … yes, yes, isn't much evidence of your lot up here except for a helicopter pilot who seems to want to fly home to mummy at the merest flash of lightning … yes, I know it's a very dangerous job … I know … anyway, we'll get back to you."

Bethany asked, "What was that all about, Sebastian?"

Before he could answer they were both aware of the unfortunate Mr Dylan, struggling back up towards them.

Breathless he said, "I've been trying to catch you!"

"Mr Dylan, just the man," said Sebastian. "The applicant from within for Mr Hill's job, if I'm not very much mistaken?"

"Correct," said Mr Dylan, looking across to Bethany for some sort of sign of affirmation, which didn't materialise.

"Well, you know those cucumbers you gave Sutcliffe permission to grow, to surprise his granddad?"

"Yes," said Mr Dylan.

"Well, his granddad will be surprised because, according to Superintendent Lockhart, they seem to have mutated into forty seven cannabis plants! A young constable found them, along with an extremely happy looking piglet, by the name of Boris, snuffling around in an out of the way, dilapidated greenhouse, by the old allotments."

"Well, at least that's one piece of good news," said Dr Sims.

"What else has gone so terribly wrong, on your watch then, Mr Dylan?"

"That's what I want to tell you. I had a call a little while ago from Sheila, at school. It's Peter and Carl; they've stolen all the rockets and pyrotechnics from the science lab!"

At that moment, as if Peter Sutcliffe had directed the coming extravaganza himself, which, indeed, he most certainly had, he pulled at the flint of his granddad's old lighter, which was all that was needed, protected by the asbestos like hands of Carl Borman and the shielding bodies of Miriam Stiff and Maxine Dalton, and caressed with a flame the one, blue fuse necessary to let a frenzy of spectacular fireworks off, launching them up, far away into the dark, stormy sky.

And, as the strains of Elton John's strident voice sang out about a lonely rocket man, lighting fuses, just like Peter, a few fields away, Françoise shrieked out, "Bloody hell!"

"The boy's a genius," cried Dave!

"Excellent!" shouted Tom, who felt a certain responsibility for the drama unfolding, due to his encouragement of Peter's improvisations around revolutionary themes.

Back on Pillory Mound, Mr Harris exclaimed, "You told us there'd be fireworks, Ms Sedgeford. But I wasn't expecting this!"

"Yes, I do love a good, old fashioned firework party," said Dr Sims.

"Well, we're so pleased you could make it," said Sebastian. "Any other day and it would have just been boring old lessons! You must come again next year!"

Great cascades of spuming colour rose up and then fell back down in the dark sky, drawing gasps of amazement from the inspectors, Bethany, Sebastian and Mr Dylan, as well as Dave, Tom and Françoise, who were still approaching Chapel Bank, running across the fields. Dave had gone ahead and Tom and Françoise stopped for a minute. They couldn't resist the temptation and, even though it was dangerous to stand under a tree in a lightning storm, it was also equally romantic; so they did and kissed each other lovingly on the lips.

"Oh! Yes!! Yesss!!! Ohhhh!!!!" cried the gathered audience and their sounds were echoed across the town, where angry drivers, stuck in the gridlock, blocked by Mr Bull's herd of Herefords, were compensated by the wonderful, unexpected display. Back at Southgreen Academy, students, teachers and teaching assistants, as well as the three other inspectors, were scrambling to get to the windows to see the breath-taking effects.

"Mr Dylan," said Bethany, "didn't you say Peter Sutcliffe was designing some pyrotechnics that would write Mr Hill's name in the sky?"

"That's what he was attempting," said the muddy Welshman, "but I must confess, I haven't seen them."

"I wonder if Mr Hill is watching now?" asked Bethany.

And indeed he was, for he and Susan Shepherd had allowed the Year 9 students that they were supervising in the gymnasium, out into the playground, as the rain had stopped. Just as they got there, the sky lit up, one letter at a time, each in a different, vibrant colour, spelling out, 'MR HILL' and then, after a pause, the fireworks continued exploding in cascading showers of words that announced that he was, 'OVER THE HILL.'

All the children laughed and Mr Hill, who was nothing if not a good sport, laughed too. This started Susan off clapping and then all the students responded with a massive round of applause, which built and continued.

Françoise cried out, "Wicked!"

Dave shouted, "Priceless!"

And then, as if Peter was offering his audience the revolutionary icing on Marie Antoinette's cake, the next tranche of fireworks exploded, again in individual letters of sparkling colour, spelling out:

'S A L A M I'

"AAHHH!!!" came the cries from miles around, as the applause in the Southgreen playground grew to a crescendo.

Even Mr Sanders and the parents and children at Brooksham Primary; likewise Mr Amyes at Bidhurst, were given a marvellous, unexpected treat, as they watched the sky exploding above them at home time.

"This is all your fault, you know," Dave told Tom.

Tom laughed with pride and said, "Yeah, great isn't it. I'll race you," and off they sped now nearing Chapel Bank.

Dr Sims and Mr Harris were delighted with what they had seen but, after the fireworks had stopped, there was an awkward anticlimactic feeling and the silence was only broken by a nervous and worried Mr Dylan who turned to Bethany and said, "Boss, it's probably not the right time, but I was wondering if you'd come to a final decision about the job?"

"I'm sorry, Mr Dylan," said Bethany, with a serious look on her face.

"Sorry?" asked Mr Dylan.

"Yes," said Bethany, now looking overly sympathetic. "I'm sorry Mr Dylan, what with all this excitement, I forgot to tell you. I let the other two candidates go at lunch time; there really was no point in continuing, as they'd covered absolutely everything most comprehensively."

"Right, boss," said Mr Dylan, now deflated.

"Evan," she said, "I don't quite know how to tell you this ..."

He prepared himself for the worst.

"The thing is," she continued, "they might have been highly qualified Oxbridge graduates but, between you and me, they were nothing but a couple of dummies!"

"You mean?"

"Yes, Mr Dylan, you are the new Head of Science at Southgreen! Congratulations!"

Mr Dylan, hugged Bethany saying, "Thank you. Oh, thank you, boss!"

Sebastian was gripped by what he was viewing through his binoculars.

"Well, at least the rozzers are there now in the Range Rover but they're not getting very far," he said, giving a running commentary on the unfolding events, as if he was covering the Grand National. "Oh, look, one of them has fallen. There are three other people approaching ... well done, yes, it's Dave Hardman and that Carter chappie with Mademoiselle Poitin ... Now they're talking to Peter and Carl." Just then the minibus pulled up and Mr Bull, Dick and Andy Bailey all got out, completely covered in mud.

"And what have you been doing?" asked Bethany.

In unison they answered, "Chasing pigs!"

"All present and correct," said Mr Bull. "As I thought, Jo Brand, Lisa Riley and old Hattie Jacques rounded most of the piglets up. Old Annie Widdecombe was found wandering around in a daze and Vanessa Feltz was nowhere to be seen. She trotted back twenty minutes later, from the depths of Bidhurst Woods, with a spring in her step and looking very pleased with herself, only to find a wild sow tenderly nursing her littl'uns."

"Très bien, Mademoiselle," said Sebastian, enjoying his enforced voyeurism, "She seems to be persuading Peter to give himself up. Mr Carter's chipping in, as well. Yes, well done, they've done it ... they're walking down the hill, oh and the rozzers are there now ... they've spread-eagled Sutcliffe and Borman over the bonnet of the Range Rover ... and now ... they're cuffing the lot of them ... Oh, now Dave Hardman's remonstrating with the police ... yes, and they're removing the cuffs ... oh, no, now Borman's giving the officer the zeig heil routine ... he's being cuffed again and Miriam Stiff's shouting at the policemen. Now, she's laid hands on Carl and he's grabbed hold of her –" here Sebastian stopped abruptly, before he said with total disgust, "and they're snogging!"

There was a momentary pause before Bethany said, "Well, Dr Sims and Mr Harris, how have you enjoyed your day at Southgreen?"

She looked them both in the eye. They stared at each other and then both turned back to her, speechless.

♦ ♦ ♦

At 8.15 the next morning Helga arrived in the staff room to find Dave Hardman, who was still marking exam papers.

"Morning Dave," she said.

"Morning Helga," Dave replied, not looking up.

She entered her office and hung up her jacket. Then she moved the framed photograph of her daughters, kissed it and started to remove the mic from where Mr Dylan had secured it with a small piece of tape. That done she removed the wire from the desk leg and from underneath the carpet that led to the door to Bethany's part of the office. She cut the wire and rolled it up, placing it in a plastic carrier bag. She then got a large post-it note and wrote on it, putting it in the bag and sticking it to the wire. Once completed she crossed to Bethany's office, knocked on the door and, when there was no reply, she entered, leaving the bag on the Principal's desk before returning to her office and putting the kettle on.

A few minutes later, Bethany entered her office from the corridor. Immediately she saw the plastic bag on her desk and opened it, removing the mic and the wire and picking up the post-it note. She read it. It said, 'You're just going to have to put up with me. I'm returning your bugging equipment. Mr Harris knows all about it. I haven't decided yet whether to take it any further.' Bethany looked up and took a moment, as she thought about the best course of action. Then she called out, as loudly as possible, "Morning Helga!" A few seconds elapsed before Helga replied, just as loudly, "Morning Bethany!"

♦ ♦ ♦

At the morning briefing, Sebastian was in full flow. "Carl Borman has been charged with taking and driving away a motor vehicle, driving without a license, driving without insurance, causing a breach of the peace and the theft of farm animals. Peter Sutcliffe, who is contrition itself, particularly because of indirectly causing the death of four cockerels, has been charged with all of the above and cultivating 47 cannabis plants. Amazingly and loyally, old Mr Sutcliffe has come to his grandson's defence by willingly admitting to police that he smoked cannabis to ease the symptoms of his rheumatoid arthritis and Peter was simply fulfilling the role of the kind apothecary. Also, both our precious animals and the fireworks were school property, along with the vehicle and trailer. The boss has provisional permission from the fully informed governors not to press charges on these matters. Anyway, I think you'll all agree it was a bloody good display. Eh, Mr Hill?"

Mr Hill was thoroughly exhausted from his sterling efforts the previous day. After making an early morning coffee he had settled into his chair and fallen into a deep sleep that he couldn't be wakened from. Mr Dylan, buoyed by his new status, happily spoke on his behalf.

"Mr Hill told me that, although he didn't condone his criminal behaviour, he thought Peter Sutcliffe's understanding of the chemistry involved in making such novel pyrotechnics was very impressive. He was sure he'd gain an A* in his GCSE exams next year."

Susan Shepherd was about to lead another round of applause but felt better of it, stopped after the first clap and then blushed and covered her face.

"Have the girls been charged with anything, Mr Swinton?" asked Françoise.

"Thank you, Mademoiselle Poitin and, may I say, the police were very appreciative of the way you, in particular, talked Robespierre, Che Guevara and their motley crew into surrendering. Amazingly, Maxine Dalton and Miriam Stiff have not been charged with any offence though, I must say, personally, watching Miriam Stiff snogging Carl Borman through binoculars was pretty offensive! On a lighter note, staff will want to welcome back Linda Baker, after her absence and will notice, I expect, a small protuberance growing beneath her attire, which is all down to Mr Bailey in PE."

Linda had a broad smile on her face and was blooming early into her second trimester. She'd got over the morning sickness and wasn't depressed anymore. She sat holding hands with Andy Bailey, who had finally met his match. That there was a long queue of women who wouldn't want to swap with her, knowing Andy's promiscuous ways, didn't bother her at all. His vanity at the thought of a little boy, made in his own image, had done the trick and she was prepared to believe that he was a changed man.

"Continuing to accentuate the positive," said Sebastian, "staff will be delighted to know that our temporary drama teacher, Mr Carter who, I have to say, was specifically picked out by the inspectors for the quality of his teaching, will unfortunately not be back next term, as he will follow up his leading role as a sex deviant in the 'Stranger Danger' campaign, by taking the part of Danny in 'Night Must Fall,' by Emlyn Williams, at Dundee Rep. Remind us again about the character, Mr Carter?"

"A bit different from my other parts, Mr Swinton. He just happens to be a psychopathic axe murderer."

They were becoming a veritable double act, as the entire staff room erupted in raucous laughter. Susan Shepherd couldn't contain herself and started to applaud. Everybody else did too and now it was Tom's turn to blush, though he behaved just like any thespian would and stood up to take a bow.

"Just one last thing," said Sebastian. "The boss has erred on the side of caution and excluded all the culprits up to, but not including, the last day of term, when they will return with a clean slate. We must remember that, despite their delinquent behaviour, their GCSE year starts in September."

"If I could butt in, Sebastian," said Bethany. "Just to let you all know that, although the official report is still under wraps, Mr

Harris, Dr Sims and their team were very impressed by what they saw and said that we all coped with extremely difficult and exceptional circumstances in the most professional manner. Mr Harris was struck with the rapport between staff and students and singled out for special praise the support staff along with Mademoiselle Poitin, Mr Carter and Mr Hardman, particularly for the exemplary way those three teachers dealt with yesterday's events on Chapel Bank. You'll all be delighted to know that they won't be returning in the near future."

There were now cheers from everybody and much self-congratulation, though Dave Hardman was not celebrating. He thought they'd had a lucky escape and that after the temporary liberation of the farm animals, it would have been very difficult for the inspectors to be critical. Despite what appeared to be great praise from Mr Harris and Dr Sims, he was wondering how Peter Sutcliffe, who had been reviled by the vast majority of staff, ever since his arrival at Southgreen, could have called into question the very reason for the school's existence. The farm, Bethany had said, was the school's 'jewel in the crown' but Peter, with the help of three other, underachieving fifteen year olds, had undermined the whole system of governance in a manner that Guy Fawkes would have been proud of.

♦ ♦ ♦

The Summer Fair, the following Friday, went off without the climax that everybody had been expecting, as Peter Sutcliffe had literally stolen its thunder by his exhilarating and spectacular display of exploding and colourful pyrotechnics a few days before.

Nevertheless, much hilarity occurred and Susan Shepherd and her partner Angela suffered the most dreadful indignity, being locked in the stocks together, while wet sponges and water filled balloons were hurled at them. Some over excited Year Nines then took advantage of the fact that Mr Hill, who was supposed to be overseeing the stocks, in order that due decorum be observed, had fallen fast asleep in his director's chair. They began by throwing over-ripe tomatoes and grapes, several of which hit both Susan and Angela, but when they started throwing eggs they'd nicked from the farm stall, and pieces of lemon they'd taken from the jugs of sangria that the adults were drinking in the refreshments' tent, Mr Dylan had to step in to release the unfortunate couple. Despite this generosity, he couldn't forget the look in Susan's eyes when she had hurled a lump of blu tack at him, on the morning of his interview, so he showed little sympathy, as poor Susan was now smarting from an egg that had hit her clean on the chin and a small piece of lemon, along with some eggshell that had lodged in her left eye. This didn't stop her however from enjoying what was going to be another momentous night, where her reputation would soar to even greater heights.

Once the tears, which the citric acid had caused her to shed, had dried, and Angela had removed the offending eggshell, Susan changed into her glad rags, like Cinderella, back combed her blonde hair and covered her eye lashes and lids in black mascara and eye shadow. She then made her way to the Karaoke tent where she not only reprised her rendition of 'I only want to be with you,' this time before an audience of both adults and children, but then followed it up with several more Dusty Springfield songs.

Tom and Françoise were secretly canoodling in a corner of the tent, and Françoise got tearful when Susan sang, 'If you go away,' since Tom was soon to be off to Scotland to play the axe killer. He consoled her however with a surreptitious kiss and told her he wouldn't be in Scotland for long and, anyway, she could come and visit him. Then, when Susan sang, 'You don't have to say you love me,' he led her out behind the tent where, unseen by others, he kissed her passionately, before telling her that he did indeed love her. She smiled, returning the sentiment and the kiss and, as the applause for Susan and cries of "More" rang out from the crowd, they returned to the karaoke tent, where the once timid teaching assistant blew them all away with her cover of 'Son of a Preacher Man.'

In another part of the field people had been rolling balls along the ground or lobbing them into a board full of arched holes. Each hole had a number above it. If you rolled the ball through the hole you scored the relevant number. Each player had five balls which cost 50p. The highest number on the board was six, meaning the maximum total possible was thirty. The person with the highest score at the end of the evening won a pig from the farm.

Mr Bull liked to try his luck at this, as it meant that this little piggy stayed at home where it belonged, though the winner had the option of handing the animal straight back to the farm and exchanging it for a top raffle prize. Brian had won the pig at the Summer Fair for the previous three years and, nearing the end of the competition, before the raffle, he had the highest score of twenty eight, having rolled four sixes and a four. He was one in front of Mr Sanders, the Head of Brooksham Primary, who'd had the shocking experience of an electric fence almost welding his testicles to an iron gate, some weeks before. Mr Sanders however was nothing if not determined. A crowd, including both Bethany and Helga, who'd both had quite a few glasses of sangria, gathered around the area. Mr Sanders had watched other players rolling the balls and, the ground being uneven, had seen them perform badly, getting very low scores. Consequently, he had developed a lob throw which tried to take the unpredictability of the ground out of the equation, and landed the ball directly in front of the hole. It was all about finding the right trajectory. His first ball went straight into the hole marked with a 'six.' He tried to repeat the throws in quick succession, as this had worked before. It did again and the next three throws all scored six. He was just about to throw his last ball when Helga, rather loudly and drunkenly said, "Come on, Mr Sanders, smash it!" This distracted him but he stopped just in time, composed himself and lobbed the ball again, straight into the hole marked 'six.' He'd done it! He'd scored the maximum, beaten Mr Bull and won!

All that remained was for the raffle to be drawn and prizes to be awarded. Several parents and their children won boxes of chocolates and bottles of various varieties of alcohol and some teachers and teaching assistants were in luck too. Susan Shepherd won a ten pound Boots voucher, which she would spend on mascara and make up, to help her next appearance as Dusty look even more realistic. Mr Dylan won a gift voucher for the same amount and vowed to replace his Bugs Bunny tie which, although it had brought him good luck, was rather the worse for wear and, despite washing on the 'heavy stains' cycle (which hadn't been a good idea) still smelled of cow dung. Andy Bailey also won a giant box of jelly babies, which was appropriate, since he was soon to have a small baby boy of his own. He collected it, holding hands with Linda Baker and they held it aloft like a trophy, though Randy Andy was the only real trophy that Linda cared about winning.

There was only one more prize to announce and, after a short speech from Bethany, Mr Bull presented Mr Sanders with a piglet that went by the name of Boris. He had grown significantly since their last encounter, but Mr Sanders was still able to hold him in his arms and feed him with the bottle that Mr Bull had passed to him. Then he announced that he was going to keep Boris, and take him back to be reared at Brooksham Primary, which would encourage the children to choose a secondary school that had a farm. While the crowd applauded, Bethany smiled at Helga and said, "See, Helga, what did I tell you? It's all a numbers game!"

◆ ◆ ◆

The staff room clock read 15.40 on Tuesday, 21st July. It was empty however except for one person, namely, Mr Hill. This being his final day, he had decided not to watch the children leaving on the coaches, as it would simply be too much for him. That's where the rest of the staff were now. In the staff room the tables were laid out with trays of nibbles for the final celebration of the year, and Mr Hill knew that, as he was retiring, he was going to be given the statutory leaving present and would probably be asked to make a speech. He was exhausted from his efforts over the final week however and, if the truth be known, he'd been feeling particularly fragile and needed an invigorating dose of caffeine, to ensure that he kept awake. So he pinched a few of his favourite Cheeselets from a plate of nibbles, made himself an espresso and sat down in his reclining chair. No sooner than his head had hit the head rest however, he fell into a deep sleep, before a sip of strong coffee had passed his lips.

Sebastian entered, looking chirpy, saying, "It's the very best moment of the year for me. I don't know why it is, but waving the pupils off on the coaches, at the butt end of July, encapsulates a meaning that's difficult to express in words."

"I've always found 'bugger off' works quite well," said Dave.

"Yes, well you're just a fucking cynic, Dave," said Sebastian, before crossing to Françoise and saying, "returning to the boyfriend in France during the holidays, Mademoiselle Poitin?"

"No, I don't have a boyfriend in France, Basil."

"And where might he be then?"

"Scotland," said Françoise, as Bethany entered from her office.

"You wanna watch the Scots," said Sebastian, "you never know what they've got under their –"

"Sebastian," said Bethany, forcefully, cutting him off. "I'm just going to powder my nose and then we'll start the proceedings. I've got a plane to catch to Bermuda in four hours' time."

♦ ♦ ♦

Mr Hill would be present at the end of year get together for the last time and since this was the title of her favourite Rolling Stones' song Helga was playing it on the CD player, in his honour. She was untouchable now and enjoyed the feeling, having secured her position; Mr Harris being fully aware of exactly what had gone on. It was entirely her decision, if she wanted to take the bugging matter further. She was invulnerable. She had won.

Bethany came in and said, "Do I look, okay?"

"Very presentable, I'd say."

"Thank you, Helga. Good choice of music."

"Thank you, Bethany. That's what I thought; being Mr Hill's last day."

"Exactly. I hope you have a good holiday in Lanzarote."

"Why ever do you think I'm going there?" asked Helga.

Bethany looked sheepish.

"Oh, of course. How silly of me," said Helga, remembering her Oscar winning performance, "that was just for the imaginary Mr Harris's benefit. I wasn't really talking to anyone. I'm taking the girls to visit my sister in Bognor Regis."

"Well, have a lovely time there," said Bethany. "Maybe we can start next term with a clean slate?"

"Maybe," said Helga, who wouldn't relinquish her new found control that easily. "Well come on. You've got that plane to catch to Bermuda."

♦ ♦ ♦

The staff room was packed with staff eating nibbles and toasting the end of term with glasses of sparkling wine. Bethany had congratulated them all on their performance and was still trying to convince them that Southgreen Academy was an improving school. This was an opinion that had very little support, because most of the staff thought it was the same as it always had been which was 'challenging,' to say the least. Taking the school out of local authority control, changing the name of the school to Southgreen Academy and calling the new Head Teacher, The Principal, had made not the slightest difference. She was nearing the end of her speech.

"And just one last thing," she said. "I'm sure all the staff would like to congratulate Dick Fenwick in PE on his engagement to Julia Lyons. Staff will remember that Julia was on placement here during terms four and five. Dick will also be taking on the role of Acting Head of PE when Andy Bailey is on special paternity leave. And now we come to the main reason why we are all gathered here this afternoon, so, without further ado, I'm handing you over to our next Head of Science, Evan Dylan."

Mr Dylan stood up and cleared his throat, as if he were going to launch into a chorus of 'Bread of Heaven' which, thankfully, he didn't. He started slowly and seriously saying, "Colleagues, I have been at Southgreen now for nine years and am looking forward to my new responsibilities, but I couldn't have got to where I am today without the help and support of our very own Mr Hill." He stopped and looked over to Mr Hill, whom no one had been able to wake from his deep slumber. He waited to see if he would come round, but he didn't. Nobody knew what to do except Susan Shepherd who, very quietly, stood up and moved close to Mr Hill's chair. She leaned towards him and whispered in his ear, immediately jumping back, which was sensible, as Mr Hill lashed out at her and sat bolt upright saying, "Where, where?" Of course Susan had repeated her method of rousing him when the fire alarm had been set off, exactly a week ago. The words she had whispered then, 'Fire, fire,' had worked for a second time.

"I'm terribly sorry, I must have dropped off," said the retiring Mr Hill, stifling a yawn.

"That's quite alright," said Bethany, "Mr Dylan has been singing your praises. Please continue, Evan."

"As I was about to say, Mr Hill has been a tower of strength at this school for over forty long years. His knowledge of science is unsurpassed in my book. Oh, you can talk of string theory, astrophysics, quantum mechanics, the selfish gene; Stephen Hawking, Albert Einstein, Richard Dawkins and the rest, but when it comes to sheer communication skills, Mr Hill is par excellence in my book." From behind a chair, hidden from view, Mr Dylan retrieved a large box, beautifully wrapped in gold paper and silver ribbon. At the same time, Susan Shepherd produced an enormous bouquet of flowers. "I offer him now this final present, on behalf of all the staff. He is retiring today after a lifetime of teaching and, with the utmost humility and respect, I ask him now to say a few words to us all. Mr Hill."

Mr Hill slowly stood up to face his audience. He paused for a few seconds to compose himself and then started, carefully choosing his words. "It is humbling to stand here at last, in front of my friends and colleagues. I must thank my deputy and the next Head of Science at Southgreen, for his kind words, the beautiful flowers - thank you too, Susan - Chrysanthemums, my favourite - and this wonderful present, which I will open later."

"I will try and be brief. I started teaching in 1966, the year England won the World Cup, at a time when everything was possible. To try to describe the unbridled optimism that existed then, would seem ridiculous to people today but then we did, indeed, want to change the world. We have failed. To change the world there are only two things, in my estimation, that need to be realised. They are that all people are equal and equality is precious and needs defending at all cost and, secondly, that there are innumerable ways of achieving the realisation of humanity's great goals."

"First, and I hope my grammar is correct, Mr Hardman, I always wanted to impart my great love of science to others. I knew that all of the important questions about life and the universe could be answered, if only we allowed everybody to have equal access to those questions and equal means to discover the answers. Very soon however, I realised that this wasn't the case. There is no equality. People don't have equal access; they don't have equal means. Most of the great public institutions, as well as many of our big corporations and companies, are top heavy with people who were privately educated, who had greater access and means to gain access to the corridors of influence and power than the rest of us. Indeed, halfway through the first decade of the twenty first century we have a Prime Minister who went to an expensive private school. His parents were in a position to buy him a privileged education. And he, supposedly, adheres to the principals of social justice."

"Soon after I started teaching, I became aware that, despite my great love of science, there were too many people who were saying,

'No, you don't want to teach it like that, you want to teach it like this.'"

"Like Harry Enfield," shouted Dave.

"Yes, exactly, but it's the politicians who are the comedians! They say, 'no, teach it like this' or a few years later they say, 'no, that was wrong, teach it like this,' or, 'if we want to stoke the fires of industry we need to be teaching like this' and, quite frankly, none of them know what they're really talking about! What riles me is that these people who, without any real knowledge, tell me I should be teaching this way or that way, don't understand at all! And never have! Most of them haven't spent any time with children! They're simple spouting the current dogma, insisting they're 'raising standards' and giving parents 'choice,' when what they're actually doing is constantly moving the goalposts and heaping endless bureaucracy onto a completely overworked and demoralised workforce."

At this point there was a spontaneous round of applause, led by Dave, but Mr Hill, who had never been seen so animated, and who was becoming visibly agitated and not a little short of breath, stopped them, waving his hands, saying, "And until we get away from this, we'll never achieve any real success. I mean you don't get them telling surgeons that they should do their operations this way or that way! It's nonsense! But with teachers, as far back as I can remember, these idiots seem to be allowed to tell us how to do our jobs!"

He stopped for a few seconds to catch his breath and then said, "Anyway, I've gone on far too long but I felt I just had to get these thoughts off my chest on this, my final day at Southgreen. So, without further ado, and with a last thank you to all the wonderful teachers, assistants and students that I've had contact with, over all these years, I'd just like to say ... I'm sorry ... I'm really ... very ... very sorry ... but I'm not feeling at all well!"

With these final words, Mr Hill's eyes started rolling backwards and he grabbed hold of the arm of his chair for support but it wasn't enough to steady him. It gave way and he collapsed and fell heavily to the floor. Great gasps and shrieks of shock were heard and staff surrounded Mr Hill's prone and immovable body.

"I don't believe it," cried Sebastian.

"Let me through," said Mr Dylan, "I'm a trained first aider."

"Give him air," said Bethany.

"Move back for Christ's sake!" shouted Dave, trying to get people to do just that.

"Phone an ambulance someone," implored Tom.

"I'm doing it now," said Sebastian, getting out his mobile.

Mr Dylan immediately looked for signs of life which weren't apparent. He checked that Mr Hill's airway wasn't obstructed, pinched his nose, tilted his head back, giving him mouth to mouth resuscitation and then started pounding his chest. Françoise knelt beside him to help and felt for a pulse, whilst trying to establish if he was breathing.

Mr Dylan gave more chest compressions as Bethany said, "This can't be happening!" But it was and Françoise said, "He's not breathing," while Mr Dylan pumped his chest, forcibly pressing his two hands against his sternum, saying, "We're losing him, boss."

And losing him they were, despite their heroic efforts. The ambulance arrived within ten minutes, during which time Mr Dylan and Françoise continued with chest compressions and mouth to mouth resuscitation. Susan Shepherd took turns with them, as she was also a trained first aider, but the rest of the staff were encouraged to vacate the staff room, and were told that they would be kept informed and it would be best if they went home. They were all in state of profound distress. After a few minutes of conversations about what they had just witnessed, most of them headed for the car park and their cars. Some of them saw the ambulance arrive and two paramedics rushing to the aid of poor Mr Hill.

They established immediately that he was in cardiac arrest and used the defibrillator, shocking his heart. They had to shock him twice and when they felt a faint pulse they administered the necessary anti-clotting drugs and saline solution and quickly got him onto the trolley and dashed him to the ambulance.

Bethany entrusted Sebastian and Mr Dylan to follow them to the hospital; she still had a plane to catch. Very soon the school was empty, except for Mr Bull, who was tending to the cows, Mr Doyle, who was in his workshop and the two cleaners.

At the hospital, the A&E doctors took over, but unfortunately Mr Hill went into cardiac arrest again, and despite doing everything possible, they could not revive him. Time of death was certified at 17.05.

Fifteen minutes before this terrible event took place, back at Southgreen Academy, Doreen, the cleaner, was clearing up the staff room, wiping down the tables and emptying the bins. She washed up dirty crockery in the kitchen area and hung the mugs on their hooks. There was one with the soon to be deceased, Head of Science's name on. She picked up the gold wrapped present and placed it on Mr Hill's reclining chair, next to the broken arm and chrysanthemums. Then she hoovered. As she was finishing, over the noise, she heard someone shouting from outside in the corridor. She switched off the hoover and unplugged it. The voice from the corridor shouted again, "Is anybody there?" Doreen opened the main door and said, "No, luvvie, they've all gone." Then she picked up the hoover and left.

A minute or so later, Peter Sutcliffe made his way along the corridor, making sure that no one had seen him, and slowly opened the main staff room door. He entered. He had never stepped foot inside before. Of course he had spent many hours, over the months and years, in the corridor outside, asking to see various teachers to discuss something he considered to be of the utmost importance but, invariably, he'd been told to go away or, quite often, been chastised or even, on occasion, humiliated. A few teachers had been helpful and sometimes even kind, but still he felt there'd always been a barrier between them and him.

He walked over to the door that said, 'Principal's Office' and entered. He looked around and, after a moment, crossed into Ms Sedgeford's part of the office, through the adjoining door. It was unremarkable. He looked into the mirror. His red hair had grown and bleached lighter in the hot, July weather. He noticed several spots on his face and one in particular that was ripe and fit to burst. He got closer to the mirror and squeezed the spot between his thumb and his index finger. The pale, yellow puss shot onto the glass. He looked around for a tissue, to wipe it away with, but thought better of it. He would leave it there like an animal marking its territory. Then he returned to the staff room.

He had noticed the ambulance arrive earlier and, taking care not to be seen, he'd overheard a conversation, between two teachers, about what had occurred. He had no idea however of the final, tragic outcome that was still yet to happen. He looked across to see the gold wrapped present next to the chrysanthemums, on Mr Hill's recliner. It resembled a shrine. He had learnt that chrysanthemums were often considered flowers of death. He hoped, sincerely, that Mr Hill would survive. Whatever happened, at that moment, Peter resolved to get an A* next year, in his GCSE Chemistry. He was curious to see what was inside the wrapped present but had no intention of defiling it. He crossed over and carefully unstuck one piece of tape and gently lifted the gold paper. He could see that beneath was an espresso, coffee making machine. He re-stuck the tape, his curiosity sated, sat down in a chair opposite and got out his iPod.

Over recent weeks he'd become a big fan of Billy Bragg, after one of his chats with his new found friend, Dave. He plugged in his ear phones to listen. Then he picked up a copy of the Times Educational Supplement which was lying on the table in front of him. He rested it on his knees and, from his pocket, took out a brown paper bag. Although the police had found forty seven cannabis plants in the old, dilapidated greenhouse, most of them were only at the sapling stage. He'd already harvested three others, from an earlier crop, which were far more substantial and had produced large, beautiful green and purple buds with a sweet, pungent smell. He had shared the contents with his granddad, aka Peter Sutcliffe, who had been telling the truth to the police about his rheumatoid arthritis but who had, anyway, smoked cannabis ever since his days in the merchant navy. He thought the world of his grandson. He knew that Peter junior was a highly intelligent and clever young man with a great future in front of him.

Peter took out his King Size Rizla papers and proceeded to roll a joint of his pure, personally cultivated, home grown grass. When he had finished, he took out his granddad's fisherman's lighter, flicked the flint and lit the spliff. He took a deep draw and held the smoke in his young lungs for several seconds.

He thought of the events of the past few weeks and was proud of his achievements, though he felt guilty about the death of the four cockerels. He'd already made plans to hand leaflets out, lobbying against the fried chicken takeaway, run by the man who'd wielded the axe.

He thought of the past four years at Southgreen. All he had ever wanted was to enquire. To ask brilliant questions and to find brilliant answers. That's why he had spent so much time in the corridor but, over time, it had alienated him from his teachers and peers.

Peter looked across to the staff room clock and, as he did so, the final digit moved and the time changed from 17.04 to 17.05. He would have to go very soon or he'd be found out, so he took another large drag on the joint and, as Billy Bragg's voice rang out, the final words of the great Blake hymn, 'Jerusalem,' resounded in his ears.

'I will not cease from mental fight,
Nor shall my sword sleep in my hand,
Till we have built Jerusalem
In England's green and pleasant land.'

Peter Sutcliffe had had his way and won the day. He resolved that he would no longer be ignored, waiting in the corridor. He was now 'lord of all he surveyed.'